just once more

just once more

escape to new zealand, book seven

ROSALIND JAMES

author's note

The Blues, Hurricanes, and All Blacks are actual rugby teams. However, this is a work of fiction. Names, characters, places, and incidents are products of the author's imagination or are used fictitiously and are not to be construed as real. Any resemblance to actual events or persons, living or dead, is entirely coincidental.

table of contents

new zealand map

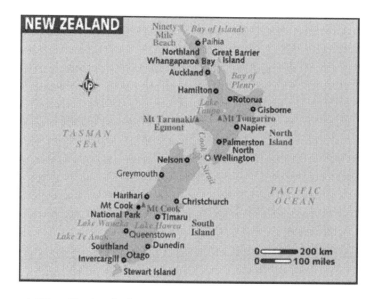

A New Zealand glossary appears at the end of this book.

cast of characters

(In order of appearance)

Sir Andrew (Drew) Callahan (36), Lady Hannah Montgomery Callahan (35). Papamoa (suburb of Tauranga). JUST THIS ONCE. Drew: much-acclaimed longtime captain and No. 6 (blindside flanker) for the Auckland Blues and All Blacks; now retired from playing and head coach of the Bay of Plenty (professional) provincial rugby team. Hannah: marketing executive for 2nd Hemisphere clothing firm. Parents of Jack (4-1/2) and Grace (18 months); new baby due in two weeks.

Helen Callahan; Sam Callahan, Te Kuiti. JUST THIS ONCE. Drew's mother and father.

Liam (Mako) Mahaka (29), Kristen Montgomery Mahaka (32), Wellington. JUST MY LUCK. Liam: No. 2 (hooker) for the Wellington Hurricanes and All Blacks. Kristen: Hannah's younger sister, and a buyer for a Wellington department store. Parents of a baby due in three weeks.

Finn Douglas (37), Jenna McKnight Douglas (33), Auckland. JUST FOR NOW. Finn: former No. 8 for the Auckland Blues and All Blacks; now retired from playing and serving as strength and conditioning coach for the

Blues. Jenna: former Year 1 teacher. Parents of Sophie (10), Harry (8), Lily (2-1/2), and a new baby due in two months.

Hugh Latimer (29), Jocelyn (Josie) Pae Ata (31), Auckland. JUST NOT MINE. Hugh: No. 7 (openside flanker) for the Auckland Blues and All Blacks. Josie: TV star. Getting married in a few days; parenting Hugh's half-siblings, Amelia (13) and Charlie (9).

Hemi Ranapia (36), Reka Harata Ranapia (35), Papamoa. JUST FOR YOU. Hemi: former No. 10 (first-five) for the Auckland Blues and All Blacks; now retired from playing and serving as backs coach for Bay of Plenty. Reka: former kindy teacher and mum to their four children: Ariana (11), Jamie (9), Luke (6), and Anika (2-1/2).

Koti James (32), Kate Lamonica James (31), Auckland. JUST GOOD FRIENDS. Koti: No. 13 (centre) for the Auckland Blues and All Blacks). Kate: accountant for the Blues team. Parents of Maia (20 months).

Dominic (Nic) Wilkinson (Nico) (31), Emma Martens Wilkinson (30), Auckland. JUST FOR FUN. Nic: No. 15 (fullback) for the Auckland Blues and All Blacks. Emma: knitwear designer for 2nd Hemisphere. Parents of Zack (8) and George (11 months).

Sarah, Motueka. JUST FOR NOW. Finn's sister.

Nate Torrance (Toro) (30), Allison (Ally) Villiers (29), Wellington. JUST MY LUCK. Nate: Captain of the Wellington Hurricanes and, for the past two years, successor to Drew as captain of the All Blacks; No. 9 (halfback). Ally: rock climbing and kayaking instructor/guide. Became engaged a week before this story begins.

George Wilkinson, Tauranga. JUST FOR FUN. Nic's father.

Arama Pae Ata, Katikati. JUST NOT MINE. Josie's mother.

in the tunnel

♡

Drew Callahan sat bolt upright in the dark, his heart hammering, his body wet with cold sweat.

"Shit."

It was nothing more than an explosion of breath, but it woke Hannah anyway.

"Drew?" She struggled to heave her body up, and his arm went out reflexively to support her. "Is something wrong?"

"Nah." He had himself back under control now, his galloping heart finally slowing. He lay back down, pulled her gently along with him. "A bad dream, that's all. You OK, though? Baby not coming or anything?"

"What?" She still sounded sleepy. "Of course not. I'd have woken you up. Why?"

He shrugged, tried to shove the dream aside. Its dark tendrils lingered despite his efforts, sticky cobwebs of fear and dread brushing across his mind. "Just a bad dream. Sorry to wake you. I know sleep's coming hard now."

"What kind of dream?" She settled herself a little more comfortably on her side, put a hand onto his chest and stroked him there. The touch of her hand, the sound of her voice began to smooth the jagged edges left by the nightmare. His muscles released some of their tension, his body settling into the mattress.

"People who tell their dreams, gah." He felt nothing but foolish now. "Anything more annoying than that? Never mind. Doesn't matter."

"Tell me. Because it scared you. Your heart's still beating so hard."

He tried to laugh. "Can't hide anything from you, I guess. OK. It was...I was in this...tunnel. With you. And somebody was coming. I couldn't quite hear, but I could tell. Somebody who meant to hurt us, I knew that."

Because he had known. He'd known it for sure, and it had scared the shit out of him. Not for him. For her.

"I was waiting," he went on. "Couldn't stand up— too low. Too narrow. In this little space, with somebody coming. Crouched down in the pitch black, listening and waiting, seconds going by, holding my breath so I could hear him breathe."

He stopped, forced himself to relax again, but the tension took hold all the same. "And then I felt him come, just this whisper in the air, and I was grabbing for his hair. Stabbing at his eyes, punching at him in the dark as best I could, trying to bang him into the rocks, and he was fighting back. Fighting so hard. He was so strong, and I was scared..." He swallowed, the fear gaining the upper hand again, tightening his muscles, shortening his breath even as he told himself it was a dream. Only a dream. "Scared that I'd lose. Scared that he'd get through me. That he'd get through me to you."

"Sounds terrifying," she said softly. Her hand was still there, stroking over his skin. "I'll bet you saved me, though."

"No." He felt her hand still for a moment in surprise. "I mean, I did, I guess, because he was gone, and I was lying there, beat to hell from having my head bashed against the rock and that. But I'd had my hands around his throat, and I'd either killed him or he was gone, don't know which. You know, dreams. But then I was still there, in the dark, in the tunnel, and I couldn't find you. And I knew you were having the baby. Right there. I knew it, and I couldn't get there. I couldn't get to you." His body remembered exactly how it had felt. Because she was right. It had terrified him.

"Which has happened," she pointed out practically. "Twice now. Though without the tunnel, thank goodness. And I've had them all the same. I know you think you're necessary, and no question, you're pretty important at the start, aren't you?"

She was trying to tease him, doing her best to ease his unquiet mind, and he was embarrassed. She should be the one being nervous, and he should be the one doing the comforting, not the other way around.

"But when it gets to that point, you know," she reminded him, "I pretty much have to do it myself. An anxiety dream, that's all it was. But it's all right."

"Going to be there for this one all the same," he told her. "Shouldn't have missed the last one. Should never have gone, not after the first time."

"No," she said instantly. "How could we have known it would be that fast?"

Because it had been fast. Too fast. He'd been here, talking to the Bay of Plenty club about the coaching job, and she'd been back in Auckland with their three-year-old. And his mum and dad, thank God.

"It's only three hours away," she'd told him when he'd vacillated about going. "It's not going to happen faster than that, for heaven's sake. You need to talk to them, I'm not due for more than ten days, and the midwife says nothing looks imminent. Go."

So he'd gone, and once again, he hadn't made it back in time, because three hours had been too long after all. He'd broken every speed limit to get to her, and it hadn't mattered. He hadn't made it.

"It's going to be me holding your hand this time," he told her now. "Not my mum. Me. So don't be thinking you're going anywhere without me for the next couple weeks, or that I'm going anywhere without you. No arguments."

"I'll be happy to have you there holding my hand, believe me," she assured him. "I want you there. And meanwhile, I guess we probably shouldn't go caving for the next couple weeks after all. Better cancel that blackwater rafting booking, you think? Shoot. I was really looking forward to that." She still had her hand on him, and she was smiling, he could tell.

He laughed. Reluctantly, but he laughed all the same. "Stupid, I know it. It's just…" He said it, in the dark. "My biggest fear, isn't it. That I won't be able to take care of you. You and the kids."

"And you might not be able to, someday, somehow," she said, no laughter in her voice anymore. "You're not always here, even now. But I manage all the same. And I would manage. To take care of myself, and the kids too, no matter what. Don't worry, Drew. It's all right."

"I know," he said. "I know. It's just…" He rested a hand on the taut roundness of her belly. "Too close, I reckon. I'm always nervous when you're this close. It matters too much. And besides, I'm used to being able to do things, to take care of things, and when you're having the baby, I can't. So hard to know you're hurting, and not be able to help."

"Somebody said that. That when you have a child, you give a hostage to the world. When you love somebody that much."

"A hostage. Yeh." He felt his son kick under his hand, held safe there under his wife's heart, and knew how true it was. "You, and the kids."

"True for me too, you know," she said. He'd turned onto his side to face her, and he could see her now that his eyes had adjusted to the darkness. The gleam of her pale hair, her eyes on him, her face so gentle. "True for both of us. Love is a risk. But you're worth it, Drew. Always."

He did his best to speak around the lump in his throat. "Yeh. So are you."

command performance

♡

Hannah woke to find the room dark, because the shades were still drawn. She could see from the bright December light shining around their edges, though, that it was morning.

No Drew beside her. She pulled the pillow that had supported her belly out from between her legs, rolled with difficulty onto her other side, and looked at the bedside clock.

Seven-thirty. She'd slept in, and Drew had let her. She still had more than two weeks to go until the baby, but everybody who'd told her the third was harder had been right, because she was dragging. Or maybe it was just that she was thirty-five now, and pregnancy, never her easiest thing, had got even harder. She couldn't love her children more, but she sure didn't love being pregnant. And last night, she hadn't loved it at all. She'd woken, slept a little, and woken again until the wee hours of the morning. Drew's nightmare had unsettled her, maybe, or maybe it was just her back. She got up, putting a hand to it as she did, and it was an effort.

But Drew was on holiday, she had a houseful of guests, every one of whom was somebody she loved, and it was a beautiful December morning. She drew the blinds to reveal a few white clouds in the impossibly clear blue of a New Zealand sky, the grass and flax plant and palms, their fronds waving a little in the gentle breeze. And, beyond, the expansive curve of beach where sand met sea. Papamoa Beach, on the Bay of Plenty. Home.

Fifteen minutes later, she was down the wide, angular white-walled stairway of the modern house, windows streaming with light, into the gleaming stainless-steel of the kitchen, where breakfast was in full swing.

Helen, Drew's mum, had clearly been up and cooking early. Drew, his father Sam, and Hannah's brother-in-law Liam were finishing off a very full breakfast with obvious contentment. Sauteed mushrooms, tomatoes, potatoes, and all. Helen had really gone to town for "her boys."

Hannah was glad she hadn't had to do it, because even this late in her pregnancy, bacon and sausage—even the smell of them—didn't sit easily. And that was particularly true this morning.

"Morning, love," her mother-in-law said.

"Morning," Hannah said, stooping with some difficulty to give her children a somewhat messy kiss that they barely deigned to return, so intent were they on their own breakfasts. "You should have woken me, Drew. Here I am, last one down."

"Nah," he said, mopping up a last bit of yolk with a piece of toast. "Needed your rest, didn't you. Baby's going to be more trouble out than in. Rest while you can."

"How did you do, Kristen?" Hannah asked. Kristen was due only ten days after her elder sister, but of course she still looked beautiful, because it seemed that Kristen could never look anything else.

"Not too badly," Kristen said, and if a pregnant woman could truly be said to glow, she was glowing. And even that irritated Hannah this morning, which was just wrong.

"Sit and have some breakfast, love," Helen said. "Eggs? Toast? More?"

"I can get it," Hannah said automatically.

"Oh, let me spoil you, my darling," Helen said. "You know how much I enjoy it, and I'll be back with only Sam to see to soon enough." Which made Hannah a little weepy. Her emotions were out of control today, and that was the truth.

"Though I'm more trouble than three," Sam Callahan, an older and even broader version of his much-decorated son, said. "So it's not really a fair comparison."

"Rubbish," Helen said. "A bit mucky from the animals, maybe." She gave Hannah a wink.

"So," Hannah said, taking a cautious nibble at a triangle of toast from the rack, a sip of the herbal tea that Helen put in front of her. Spoiling her, as always, just as she'd said. She took a breath, another sip of tea, tried her best to sound cheerful. "We've got a big day today, don't we?"

"Yeh," Drew said. "Mako and I thought we'd start it with a visit to the gym."

That made her smile after all, her first truly genuine one of the morning. "Oh, because you need to work out. Before you go water skiing and swimming and whatever else you've got planned for today."

"Aw, that's just a bit of larking about," Liam said. "Not a real workout."

"Uh-huh," Hannah shared a look with her sister. "If you say so."

"I thought we'd take the kids," Drew said. "The other boys are bringing theirs too. Drop them in the childcare there, give you girls a break before everyone gets wet and sandy and noisy. Right, you two?"

"Yeh, Mum," Jack piped up. "We're going with Dad! And then the beach!"

"Really? Who all's going?" Hannah asked.

Drew shrugged. "Everybody. All seven of us. Toro's not arriving until later today," he reminded her, referring to his successor as captain of the All Blacks, coming in for the wedding that was the excuse for this gathering of teammates past and present.

"And everybody's bringing their kids?" Hannah asked. "Drew, the gym isn't going to be able to handle that. That's..." She paused, tried to count in her head, gave up.

"We won't take the big ones," Drew said. "Just the littlies. Only seven of them. And I already rang up," he said, cutting her off. "It's sorted. Besides, Jack's going to help look after Grace, aren't you, mate?" He gave his son's hair a rumple.

"Yeh," Jack said with enthusiasm, looking up at last from his oatmeal. "Grace and I like to play at the gym, and I'll look after her, Mum. I'm very good at looking after. Want to play in the ball pit, Gracie?" he asked his eighteen-month-old sister.

Grace, all pink cheeks, blue eyes, and pale blonde curls, looked up from the cereal she had been shoveling into her mouth with all her father's famous single-mind-edness. "Play ball!" she pronounced.

Drew laughed, leaned over and gave her a kiss on the cheek, got a messy pat from an oatmeal-smeared hand on his own chin for his trouble.

"That's my girl," he said, sitting up and wiping his face with a napkin. "Knows what's important. You and

Kristen have a…a rest or something, sweetheart. Have a nice catch-up."

"A rest?" Hannah knew she shouldn't be grumpy, but she was all the same. "I just got out of bed, Drew. I don't need a rest." She saw that Drew was showing her his Patient Face, and forced herself into a cheerfulness she didn't feel. He was doing his best to help out. Time for her to do her best too. "We'll go for a walk, Kristen, before it gets too hot? Want to?"

Kristen sighed. "She's making me exercise again," she complained to Liam.

"Good for us," Hannah said. Good for her, she hoped. She had to shake herself out of this, because she had twelve people coming to the house for dinner tonight, and even though she wouldn't be doing much of the work, the idea of it was making her feel nothing but tired and cross.

"Don't wear yourself out," Drew said, reading her mood. "Because we wouldn't want you too tired to get up on your own water skis."

"Drew, you're such a tease," his mother said fondly.

Hannah had to laugh a little. "You can tell I'm grouchy, huh? I'm sorry."

"Nah," he said, pulling her to him and giving her a kiss on the forehead. "You're entitled."

"Now you know why you were always gone when the babies were due," she said, wiping her eyes, because they were leaking again. "Much wiser."

"Down!" Grace chose this moment to announce, shoving at the tray of her high chair and wriggling.

"And that would be another no." Drew took the wet cloth from his mum and wiped down his daughter's hands and face before releasing her from her imprisonment. "Happy to be here with you, grouchy or not. Go for a walk with your sister. Have a rest. Have a swim this afternoon. Whatever it takes. Mako and I know what our part in this is, don't we, mate?"

"Not answering that," Liam said, a smile lessening the impact of the broad, much-broken nose, the cauliflower ears. "Except to say, yeh. I'm right here putting up my hand to be a supportive partner. Got my nappy-changing down. Went to the one class I was home for, took notes, did a bit of practicing with Kristen on our own, and I'm all ready to hold her hand and remind her to breathe when the time comes. Can't wait."

"Me too," Drew said. "Went to almost all of them. Extra bonus points for me, d'you reckon? Felt like a bloody fool doing all those hoo-hah breaths and panting breaths and all of that, especially with every other dad in there wanting to talk rugby, but I did it all the same. Bona fide New Age dad here. You wouldn't think you'd have to go to class to learn how to breathe, though, would you? Let alone to help somebody else breathe. Definition of an impossible task. I have a dark suspicion that they're really meant to make us boys feel prepared for something there's no preparing for."

"Hey," Hannah objected, but she couldn't help smiling, because he'd jollied her out of it, exactly as he'd meant to do. "It's harder than you think, in the heat of the moment. Easy for you to say breathing's easy. You've never tried doing it while you're...passing a watermelon."

That earned a shout of laughter from Sam. "That's about it," he told Drew. "And you're on shaky ground here. Back away slowly."

"How many times did you practice scrummaging?" Hannah went on. "You'd think you'd have known how to do that too, after about thirty years of it. And you still practiced it, just about every single day."

"Got me," Drew said with a grin. "And if you feel anything, anything at all," he said, exactly as he'd been saying for the past two weeks, "ring me. I'll be fifteen minutes away, and I'll be here in fourteen. Don't wait until you're sure. Ring me."

"Yes, sir," she sighed.

He didn't bother to answer that. "Come on, then, Mako. If you're not going to disgrace your country with that scrummaging you've probably forgotten how to do already, we'd better go give you your workout."

"Hmm. Command performance?" Hannah asked, teasing in her turn now. "You called around, and suddenly seven of you guys are going to the gym? You don't get to boss them anymore, I thought."

Drew actually looked surprised, and this time, she *was* amused. "I'm not bossing anyone. I suggested it, that's all. And if you want to talk about bossing—that's Finn's department. When you see me creeping home, a shadow of my former self—that'll be all down to him. He's going to tell me I've got soft without him there urging me on, count on it. But nah. Nothing serious. It's just for fun."

show her more

♡

He should have told Finn that, Drew thought a couple hours later, because that force of nature was his usual stern taskmaster, calling out the reps and holding the boys to good account. Drew was blowing a bit, sweating more than that by the time the two of them were in the corner of the gym, selecting dumbbells for some bicep and triceps work.

"Glad you're not on the park," Finn told his erstwhile skipper, casting a critical eye over him as they began to lift the weights that, for anybody else, would have looked impossible, but for the two of them, were just another day out. Or at least would have been a couple years ago, Drew thought grimly, determined not to betray any sign of weakness before his former teammate.

"Yeh," he said shortly, his body falling into the perfect form that came with doing this for more than twenty years, because it was your job. Your life.

"Too many nights over the game film and spreadsheets, eh," Finn said.

Drew released a quick breath of laughter. "Yeh. Probably."

"Coaching's a bigger ask than playing, I reckon," Finn said, and that was true too. "All the stress, and you can't even get out there on the paddock with the boys and bash some heads to relieve it." He offered Drew a smile that didn't mask his message one bit. "More important than ever to keep up the training, eh. All that adrenaline's got to go somewhere."

"Sure you're the conditioning coach?" Drew asked, keeping up the reps and pretending he hadn't heard. "Not auditioning for that *mental* conditioning spot? Earned your psychology diploma yet?"

Finn laughed, his gruff "huh-huh" that Drew had heard for fifteen years on the practice field, in the gym, sharing a beer, and Drew grinned back at him.

It was a relief to have the big fella with him again. Not to have to be the strongest. Not to have to be the boss, just for a few minutes. Nobody was tougher than Drew, nobody was a harder man than the skipper, or, now, the coach. Nobody but Finn.

He missed that. And the way Finn had always been there backing his skipper up, too. Wherever, whenever. At training, or before the match. At halftime in the sheds, talking to the boys. And most of all, in the heat of battle. Knowing that every opponent they faced knew that a cheap shot on Drew—and there had been enough of those—meant nearly two meters of Finn coming at you.

It wasn't just that, either. It was the way he never gave less than his utmost. Practicing as hard as he played, a towering example to the younger fellas, an intimidating figure to any unlucky soul who dared to drop his workrate. Not afraid, either, to blister the paint, to say the things that Drew's taciturn style didn't allow.

A born coach, and Drew would have loved to have had him here with him in the Bay, with him and Hemi, except that he'd never pry Finn away from the Blues, not for the step down that was provincial rugby. Finn was headed for a spot with the All Blacks, it was all but written out for him. So not now. Not yet. But someday. Someday.

"I'm keeping up," he told his former teammate now.

"Running enough?" Finn asked, not ready to let it go until he was satisfied.

"Could do more," Drew admitted.

"Then do it." Finn switched to triceps extensions, and Drew followed along automatically.

"Hannah doing all right?" Finn asked after a minute.

"Why?"

The slightest twitch of a big shoulder. "Jenna wondered. When we saw her yesterday."

"Yeh." Drew finished the set of fifteen, switched the heavy weight to the other hand and started up again. "All right, but nineteen months between these two, and Jack not five yet..." He exhaled a little harder than he strictly had to. "It wouldn't have been what we planned. Except it doesn't always go like you plan, eh."

Nothing but a nod in answer to that.

"I've been a bit worried," Drew confessed, as he never had. "She's tired, that's hard to miss. And she always gets so skinny. They're meant to get bigger all over, but she never does. Never gains enough, though she swears she's good. I always wonder if..." He stopped.

Finn looked at him. "If she's not gaining on purpose? Trying to keep her figure, not that it's possible? Or to get it back quicker afterwards?"

"Yeh," Drew said reluctantly. "Except she wouldn't, not really. Not if it weren't good for the baby. And she's not vain, never has been. I don't think she'd do that. It's just that she's all belly. It's like the baby's eating her up from inside. And this time...yeh. Especially. Not that she complains," he hastened to say. "Never. You know Hannah. But..." He exhaled. "Goes quiet, or I can tell she's getting weepy and trying to hide it."

Finn switched hands himself. "Tiring time for them," he said after a minute. "Doesn't get easier, either. Third baby, and she's a bit older than Jenna, I think. That matters, just like it does for you and me. Can't pretend it's as easy as it was in your twenties. That's a lot of stress on her body, and she takes pregnancy hard. Jenna gets more...alive with it, after she's not sick anymore. But every woman's different."

Back to the biceps again, Drew's muscles fatiguing, but keeping up with Finn, because there was no choice. "Yeh," he said. "I've got my mum here now, and that helps, but there's nobody to carry that baby for her. She feels bad she can't do more, can't do as much as usual, and that makes me..." He exhaled. "Doesn't she see I don't expect it? That nobody expects it?"

"And how's she doing...in herself?" Finn asked, with more delicacy than he customarily showed. "Scared about how she looks? You think so, don't you? That she's not sure about you?"

Drew's eyes narrowed, shot to Finn's, but the other man was concentrating on the weight clasped in his fist, the heavy bicep bulging as he lifted the dumbbell close to the shoulder, but not too close. Perfect form, as always.

"About me," Drew said flatly at last. "No. She's sure about me."

"Mate." Finn was looking at his former skipper with not one lick of deference. "She knows what's out there for you. She's not stupid."

"And she knows I wouldn't take it," Drew snapped. "Because like you said. She's not stupid." His normally controlled temper was rising, and he took it out on the movement, just as Finn had told him to. Hannah wasn't the only one on edge these days.

"She knows you wouldn't, yeh," Finn said. "Because she knows you. But she worries you want to. That you wish you could. Because she's big, and she's awkward, and she doesn't feel pretty anymore, and she's worried you aren't interested anymore."

"That's rubbish," Drew bit off. He didn't want to have this conversation. Not one bit.

"Nah. It's not. You don't think that. Course you don't. But she does. They all do. If they're used to feeling beautiful, they worry they're not anymore. And if they weren't used to feeling beautiful in the first place, they worry more. They know we care how they look, no matter what we say."

"But I like how she looks," Drew said with exasperation. "Why wouldn't I? So she's pregnant. So's Jenna. You not like how she looks?"

"Not about what you and I think," Finn said. "We love seeing them like that. You and I both know that. But they don't, not unless we tell them."

"She knows," Drew said again.

"Does she?"

Drew shrugged, kept up the rhythm. "What is this," he growled, "marriage counseling, or a workout?"

Finn shut up, and Drew switched to triceps again, lifted in silence for a minute.

"So what...do you do?" he asked reluctantly. Jenna was having Finn's fourth, after all. He'd know.

"Make her feel beautiful," Finn said, clearly having been waiting for Drew to ask. "Let her know you still think she is. Let her know you still…" He stopped. "Yeh. Well. Let her know. Show her."

"I show her," Drew said shortly, leaning over and setting the heavy dumbbell back in the rack.

"Well, mate," Finn said, shoving his own weight into its spot, those damning two spaces to the right. "Show her more."

here comes the bride

♡

"**N**ervous?" Liam glanced across at Kristen.

"Oh, no," she said automatically. "No, of course not. I'm fine."

He smiled a bit at that. "OK."

She laughed a little, wished it sounded more convincing, and scrubbed her hands over the lap of the blue paisley sundress that stretched over her taut belly. Her nervous habit, and he noticed that too.

"You've met some of them before," he reminded her. "Not too bad."

"But I haven't talked to them much," she said. "I only know Nate, really, and he's not here yet. And Drew, of course."

"Ah…yeh," Liam said. "So I'd say you're good."

"What? The captain thing?" She still felt distracted. "That matters?"

"Oh, yeh. It matters. And anyway, this'll be easier. I promise. A beach day, and more of a chance to have a chat, when you're not busy being the bride and all."

"Was I too…self-centered, you mean? At our wedding?"

He let out a breath. "No. You were the bride. That's the point, isn't it."

"Sorry." She smoothed a hand over her stomach again. For comfort, and for the pleasure of touching the place where her little girl lay, the ripple of movement along her skin that was a healthy baby getting more comfortable.

"She's dancing," she told Liam, and he smiled again.

"You know what?" she added impulsively. "However pretty she is or isn't, I'm going to love her just the same."

"Well, of course you are," he said with surprise.

She barely heard him. "Because I'm sitting here thinking that I don't look good, so nobody will like me. Well of *course* I don't look good! I'm more than eight months pregnant! Why should I worry that nobody will want to talk to me because I'm not pretty? That isn't all I am!"

She was getting heated, even though she knew he wasn't the one she had to convince. It was herself.

"No," he said calmly, pulling into the Papamoa Beach Reserve carpark, full of activity on this Sunday afternoon. "It isn't. But you're wrong, you know. You're still pretty."

"Maybe to you." She got out of the car, waited until he handed her her beach bag, leaving him to take the rest of it, to stick the beach umbrella under one arm and heft the chilly bin full of snacks. She'd have offered to carry something, but he'd just look at her with that pained resignation again and tell her no, so she didn't bother.

"To everybody," he assured her, making light of his burdens as they moved down the path onto the long, broad expanse of sand. "Pregnant pretty, but pretty all the same. But you're right. That's not what matters. That's not what all these fellas—and their partners too," he added, because he could tell, Kristen knew, that that was what was really worrying her, "are going to care about. That's not what matters, and thank God for that, or you couldn't love me. And fortunately, you don't just have a gorgeous face to offer—and a beautiful body too, pregnant or not. You have a beautiful soul as well."

♡

A *beautiful soul,* she repeated to herself as they approached the group. He thought so, and since he had a beautiful soul himself, maybe he did know. Maybe.

Hannah and Drew weren't here yet, were waiting until Gracie woke up from her morning nap, so she couldn't hide behind her sister. Not that she needed to, because it wasn't about her anyway. It was about the others. She'd stay quiet, listen, laugh at their jokes. And not being pretty, no matter what Liam said, would be better anyway. With women.

And then the first person she saw, getting up from her beach towel to greet them, made her dismiss that worry. Because, as pregnant as Kristen was, there was no contest.

Jocelyn Pae Ata. The bride in the wedding they had all gathered to celebrate, and one of New Zealand television's biggest stars.

It was easy to see why. A truly stunning face, with the velvety bronze skin, lush dark hair, and chiseled cheekbones of her Maori heritage. And a body, displayed to spectacular advantage in a red bikini, that told Kristen why Josie had been selected as a model for that sporting magazine's famous calendar, and that would surely have every single man on the beach falling over himself to get another look.

Or maybe not. Because that had to be Hugh standing up beside her. The guys never looked as big on TV as they did in person. There was no helpful contrast to normal men when they were out there on the field, that was the problem, so you didn't get the full impact.

Kristen had told Liam once that she liked him because when she was with him, nobody stared at her. Hugh had to have that effect as well, and she'd bet Josie appreciated it as much as Kristen did herself. Big, tough, and nothing but fierce, his neatly trimmed dark beard putting the finishing touch on an appearance that would have had more than the rugby players unfortunate enough to be on the other side of his punishing tackles running the other way.

Liam set down his burdens, made the introductions, gave Josie a kiss on the cheek, then greeted Hugh with a quick embrace, a clap on the back that told Kristen how glad he was to see him, even though they'd been together on the All Blacks' European tour until just a few weeks ago.

"Two days to go, eh. Holding up all right?" Liam asked the two of them. "Getting married at the marae's an adventure in itself. Least Kristen probably thought so."

"Oh, no," Kristen objected. "An adventure, maybe, but it was wonderful."

Exactly the wedding she'd always dreamed of, the one she hadn't had the first time around. Family. Closeness. Love, the real kind. The right kind. And Liam, with Nate by his side, standing and waiting for her at the front of the big room with its ornate carvings, its intricately woven flax panels.

Standing in the building that was more important to him than any other, and letting her know that she was just that important too. Watching her walk to him, every line of his broad body and beloved, battered face telling her how much he wanted her to do it, how much he needed to be right here, doing exactly this. Taking her hand in his, and marrying her.

"For you, I hope it was wonderful," Liam told her. "But then, my family was nothing but rapt to have you, and no worries that you weren't good enough for me. More the other way around, wasn't it. But for this ugly bugger, who knows. It's bound to be a bit more of a challenge for a Pakeha boy. Has your future father-in-law explained to you yet," he asked Hugh with a grin, "that if you treat her wrong, you'll have not just him to answer to, but her entire whanau and the ancestors as well?"

"If I remember right," Hugh said, "it was more to the point than that. Can barely recall, to tell you the truth. I was pretty terrified at the time."

"You were not," Josie said. "And he did not."

Hugh laughed. "You think not? Think I'm making that up? Trust me, I'm not making it up. Never mind. I understand it. A Dad thing, that's all."

Hugh was raising his brother and sister, Kristen remembered. Taking it seriously, she guessed.

"Where are the kids?" Liam asked, echoing her thoughts.

Hugh gestured towards the water. "Out there on the raft. No worries, Reka and Kate are out there too. The others aren't here yet. Our job to wait for you. And Hemi and Koti are putting the boat into the water." He nodded across the beach where a tractor was backing into the surf, launching Hemi's gleaming white powerboat. "Josie's keen to show me how much better she is than me at water sports. Turns out she won some sort of wakeboarding championship, back in the day." He sighed. "And I only find this out today? Too late to back out of marrying her, I reckon."

Liam smiled. "She'll be better than me too, then," he assured Hugh. "I'm not good on boats. Pity Toro isn't here, because he's the worst, bound to make us both look good. Can't float. Something about not enough body fat."

"Aw, backs," Hugh said with a shrug.

"Not an issue for us fat boys up front," Liam agreed. "That's not my problem. Got nothing to blame but my own shrinking heart."

"It means you can babysit with me," Kristen said.

"Well, yeh," Liam said. "That too."

"When's Toro coming?" Hugh asked. "Bringing his partner, right? Ally? Haven't met her yet. She'd be another one to school us, from what I hear. Some kind of sportswoman herself, eh."

"Climbing guide. And yeh, she's been known to show him up a time or two. Or more than two. Going to do it more, too, because she's his fiancée now," Liam said with satisfaction. "He did it in front of a whole crowd last weekend. Got her parents, his parents, everybody together for it. No backing out now."

"Really." Hugh laughed. "That's awesome."

"Liam," Kristen protested. "Maybe they wanted to make an announcement."

"You reckon? Oh, well. Can't be helped. If they make an announcement," he told Josie and Hugh, "do me a favor and act surprised."

Josie laughed. "I'm going for a quick swim before we get started," she said. "Anybody?"

"No, thanks," Kristen said.

"You go on," Hugh told her.

Josie tossed her sunglasses to the towel, ran down to the water with athletic grace, kept running through the shallows, and dove. And only then did Hugh stop watching her.

true confessions

♡

A couple hours later, and everyone was there on the towels, picking at the remains of their picnic lunch in the shade of three huge umbrellas.

Josie was heaps wetter, heaps sandier, and heaps happier. She'd been a bit nervous about this—well, add it to the list of things she'd been a bit nervous about. But, as it turned out, there'd been nothing to worry about.

"I'm knackered," Hugh sighed from his spot beside her. "And all right. Josie wins. I officially concede defeat. Who knew you could grab the board and do those turns in the air like that?" he complained. "That's above and beyond, surely."

"You don't win a wakeboarding contest because you can stay on the board," she said smugly. "You win it because you can do tricks. And I've got tricks."

"Yes, you do," he agreed. "I'd say you've got tricks and then some."

"But Kate didn't do badly either," she said graciously.

"No tricks," Koti's pint-sized wife said. "But I stayed on, even though it was my first time. Koti beat me for sure, but it wasn't *his* first time. Give me some practice, buddy," she told her husband with her usual outsized attitude, "and we'll see."

"Remind me never to give you any practice, then," Koti said. "And anyway, I didn't beat Josie. Hugh's right, she gets the trophy. Or an extra slice of pavlova, in this case. About all we have to offer."

"Which she won't eat," Hugh said. "Hungry all the time. That's the price you pay for this." He put a hand on her side, fingered the gold chain that hung around her hips, weighted in the middle by the end that dipped down to the top of the extremely brief bikini bottom, a straight line to glory.

Josie smiled and let him finger it. She'd known he'd love that chain.

"But at least Hemi lost too," Koti said. "That makes me feel a bit better."

Hemi laughed. "Only because I've got a wee bit of restraint. Not actually looking to knock the mother of my children into the sea."

He and Drew had taken turns giving the kids rides on the tube behind the boat, and then had taken Nic's wife Emma out, at her request. And when Reka had wanted a turn, that hadn't surprised anybody at all.

Hemi had done a few circles, crossed the wake a couple times, and Reka had held on, to the cheers of the women on the shore. And then they'd seen her swim to the boat, pull herself in, and Hemi dive over the side to climb onto the tube. Drew had moved over, Reka had taken the wheel, and...look out.

"Every single dirty maneuver a person could do," Hemi complained. "Every single one. And I held on through all of them. Until she did that circle, got that wake so high, and flipped my tube."

"A woman has few pleasures," Reka sighed. "So few simple pleasures in life. Surely flipping your hubby off his tube is one of them. One small compensation for everything we endure."

"May want to watch yourself there, my queen," Hemi said. "I have my ways of taking my revenge."

"Well," she said smugly, "there's that too."

"And now we know," Koti grinned, "how they got those four kids. Nothing like a challenge."

"I should never've fallen in love with a Maori girl, that's what it is," Hugh complained. "Notice how Emma didn't show Nico up, Josie? Rode on the tube, happy to take a nice quiet ride around the sea with Drew's steady hand on the wheel. I think she's the woman for me. Suit you, Nico?"

"No," Nic said. "Taken me all this time and another baby to get her to this point. My hard work's done. Do your own."

"To *what* point?" Emma demanded. A pretty, petite blonde in a pink bikini, she indeed didn't look like she'd be giving Nic any competition in the toughness stakes.

Hemi dropped his head in his hands and groaned. "Mate. I can't even…No. Epic fail. Do not take notes," he ordered Hugh. "Erase that one from the memory banks. That'll get you no place you want to go."

"Speaking of going," Josie said, "we should be getting back."

"Oh, not yet," Reka said. "Let the kids finish their game. Give us a chance to chat with you."

Josie glanced at the broad stretch of firm sand near the water's edge, the tide almost fully out now. Six of the older kids, a couple of extras joining in as well, were well into a cricket game. All of the older ones, in fact, except Finn's son Harry, who was helping the littlies build a sand castle nearby, showing a patience that made Josie smile, while Hannah and her quiet sister kept an eye on them.

Amelia, meanwhile, bowled a gentle ball to Hannah and Drew's son Jack, who didn't seem to need the gentleness, because even though Jack wasn't even five yet, he gave it a good whack that had the fielders running and Jack charging for the wicket. No lack of inherited athletic ability there, that was clear.

Hugh's sister looked pretty happy to her. Had been that way all day, in fact, despite a little show of sighing and flouncing around when she and Hugh had invited the kids to come along for the afternoon.

"I'll be the oldest, though," Amelia had objected, "and the other kids are so immature. Nobody else is even a *teenager*. What would I *do?*"

"Aw, come on. Just makes it more fun. Means you can be the proper little madam you are, put them all right." Hugh grinned at his sister, rumpled her hair.

She shrieked, grabbed for it. "*Hugh!* I just finally got it *right!*"

"Oh. Sorry," he said, though he didn't look all that guilt-ridden. "But you're just going to get wet anyway," he said reasonably. "Come with us, and you'll have about a minute for Ariana and Sophie to admire your new short hair and how perfectly it's…fixed, or whatever it is, and then you'll all be in the water and it'll be a lost cause anyway."

Amelia didn't hear the last part of that, because she'd already been dashing into the bathroom to restore her carefully mussed style.

Josie understood. She'd taken Amelia for the tousled shoulder-length cut a week earlier, knowing its symbolism.

That Amelia had finally given up the ballet dream, had accepted that she would never be a bun-head. The riding lessons Hugh had arranged for her had had a fair bit to do with making the change easier.

"All *right,*" Amelia said, coming back into the room. "I'll come. But don't muss me anymore, Hugh." She glared at her brother like the Drama Queen she was, and he laughed.

"No worries," he told her. "Your perfect hair is safe from me. Until you get to the beach and forget it."

Which she hadn't done, because there had been a couple of cute boys diving off the raft, and that had meant a fair amount of showing off on their part, a good bit of giggling on Amelia's and Sophie's parts, even eleven-year-old Ariana's, who had blossomed early and was already showing signs of being as pretty—and just as curvy—as her mum. The boys had joined the cricket game as well, which had Hugh, Hemi, and Finn all keeping an eye on them, and made Josie laugh to herself. Any boy looking to get close to any of those girls was going to have a job of it. Because Ariana had a Maori dad, just as Josie did herself, and as for Finn—well, Josie wouldn't want to be the boy coming to pick Sophie up for a date. And Hugh wasn't too far off in the protective ferocity department. Not any too far off at all. One look at those hard eyes, not to mention the size of him, and a boy would be thinking twice, Josie thought proudly.

"Well, I'm not really in that big a hurry to get back," she told Reka now, her attention back on the group, which, to tell the truth, she'd been more than a little nervous about joining herself. But these were Hugh's mates, and just because there were going to be *two* All Black captains at her wedding...All right, maybe it wasn't so mad to be nervous. There was celebrity, and then there was celebrity. But in the end, it had all been easy, because that was how they were. Easy.

"It would just make me jumpy," she confided to Reka. "Being back at the house. Well, jumpier. Nobody will let me do anything anyway. There's nothing my mum loves more than cooking for a crowd, and you know all the aunties are so thrilled that I've snagged a man at last, they're all pitching in as well, making sure he doesn't beg off at the last minute."

Hugh laughed from his spot on the towel beside her, his eyes more than appreciative. He hadn't got tired of looking at her, it was clear. She'd brought a cover-up, but she hadn't put it on, because the heat in his gaze sent tingles through her that told her their wedding night was going to be a special one after all these days apart, her old-fashioned parents making anything else unthinkable. And maybe they were right at that, because anticipation was definitely doing the business for her. And, unless that look in Hugh's eyes was deceiving her, for him as well.

Maybe she should be thinking more about love and marriage and less about sex, but she couldn't help it. Thinking about the wedding just made her nervous, and thinking about sex…didn't. Anyway, she wanted him, he wanted her, and wasn't that a beautiful thing?

"So, yeh," she went on, trying her best to keep it casual, "I wouldn't have enough to do. And Hugh would be helping my dad cut the grass. Although actually, he'd probably enjoy that. Always looking for an excuse to cut the grass, isn't he."

Another laugh from him, and he knew exactly what she was thinking about, she could tell. "Josie sussed that out right away," he told Reka. "Why I was always so eager to cut her grass. Get in there however I could, that was the idea. Thought I was being subtle. Turns out not."

Hemi snorted. "An openside, subtle. Yeh, right. You're about as subtle as a brick to the head, mate."

"Well," Hugh said with a satisfied sigh, stretching himself out on the towel and shoving a forearm under his neatly-cropped brown hair, "she's marrying me in two days all the same, cold feet and all. I'm going to see to it that she does. And by the time she realizes her mistake, it'll be too late. She'll just have to spend the rest of her life working on changing me."

"Nah," Josie said, but she was laughing herself now. "I like you all right the way you are."

"She says that," Hemi informed Hugh, "but she doesn't mean it. Trust me."

"I do too mean it," Josie objected.

"Now you do," Hemi said. "Let's have this conversation next year. See if you've trained him to put the seat down yet."

A shout of laughter from Hugh. "Already happened," he told Hemi. "I can aim and everything now."

"Convo's in the toilet already," Reka observed. "Boys, eh. So how *is* the prep going, Josie? Need me to come over tomorrow and lend a hand?"

It was a serious offer, Josie knew. She hadn't spent much time with Reka, given the other woman's move to Tauranga, but she already knew that much. Reka was exactly the same as her, a Maori girl from a Maori family. She didn't have to think about whether she was comfortable, not with Reka.

"Thanks," she told her, "but we're all good. Like I said. Heaps of help. Feels odd not to be doing more myself, but they say I'm the bride, meant to do…bride things. Which for me, seems to be wakeboarding. Could have done the hen party, the male strippers, but I've decided a beach full of All Blacks in their togs may just be a wee bit better. Hardly looked at Hugh once, have I. Wondering now if I should've been a little pickier, but all this lot's taken, I guess. Pity."

Hugh pulled her down with him. "Never should've invited you," he told the other men. "Whatever was I thinking? She keeps looking at Koti, she *is* going to beg off."

"Another December wedding," Koti said, ignoring that except for a twist of his beautiful mouth. Because he did have one, and Josie didn't have to want him to appreciate it. "How many of those every single year? Think everybody here got married in December, didn't we?"

He got nods of agreement in response, went on. "Rugby wedding season. And baby season following straight away, like clockwork. Who had their first one less than a year after the wedding?" he demanded, and most of the hands went up. "More like ten months for most of you randy buggers, the way I counted. Better look out, Josie. I know I was a poor performer in that regard, and Nico was pretty shocking too," he added with a dig in the ribs for his roomie. "The forwards probably have a theory about that that I'd just as soon not hear. Something about testosterone levels. I'll just state for the record here that it wasn't my fault. Some people needed a little...convincing to take the leap."

"Uh-huh," Kate said. "Blame it on me, go ahead. Because it's true," she admitted. "But all it took was one more northern Tour away from you, another romantic wedding, and I was toast, wasn't I? Or maybe that was just the Maori influence. I'm sure Josie will make sure Hugh's keeping the forwards proud."

"And as for me," Nic put in with exaggerated dignity, "I'd already made one, remember? Did it in a week, as everybody is now fully aware. And I'll have you know that I tried my hardest on the honeymoon, too." He would have said more, but Emma was laughing, blushing, pulling him down on the sand with her, and he grinned up at the assembled company from his prone position. "Never mind. We're not sharing, I guess. Think what you like."

Josie had seen Hugh sit up, had felt his hand come out for hers even as her heart had sunk, the familiar pain twisting in her chest. She looked at him, saw the acceptance in his eyes, and knew that whatever she said or didn't say would be all right with him.

She went with honesty, because she didn't want to hide this. It was too big a barrier, would sit like an invisible elephant in the room between her and Hugh's other family, this rugby family, and that meant not telling would be worse than telling.

Harden up.

"That won't be happening for us," she told Koti. "I can't have children. So..." She lifted her chin, put a brave face on it. "It won't be on Hugh."

Reka was the first to break the silence that fell at her announcement. "I'm sorry," she said gently, and Josie choked up a bit despite herself. Reka, of all people, would know exactly how much this admission had cost her. "We've been insensitive. Not thinking that it doesn't happen that easily for everybody."

"No," Josie said immediately. "Of course you haven't. How could you have known?" She was so grateful that

Hugh hadn't told his mates, or that, if he had, they'd kept the information to themselves.

Jenna, quiet until now, took her hand on her other side. "I thought that might be true for me too," she said, her gentle face conveying nothing but sympathy. "I had some problems myself. Are they...sure?"

Josie nodded. This was just about as awful as she'd expected, but it was such a relief to get it out there. "Don't have the equipment," she said, and left it at that. She felt the press of Jenna's hand, though, and knew that she really did understand everything that meant.

"Yeh, you do," Hugh said, his arm going around her. "Got the heart, haven't you. Got everything it takes to be a mum to our kids. Got everything I need."

Finn nodded soberly from Jenna's other side. "Hugh's right. A mum's a mum, and your family's your family, however it comes about. Parts or no. Jenna is Sophie and Harry's mum every bit as much as she is to the others. That's the way I see it. Seems to me you're going to be exactly the same."

"That makes it sound easy, though, Finn," Jenna said. "And it isn't easy. You don't just...adjust like that. It's so hard, when you're dealing with that. When it matters so much to you. At least it was for me. Being around babies, pregnancy. We don't have to talk about it, at least. We can stop right now." She looked around, got nods of agreement from the other women, and Josie really had put a damper on the day.

"No," she said. "No, please. Talk about it. I want to be...part of it. If it's hard—well, some things *are* hard. Everybody here probably knows that. That doesn't mean I have to run away, or that I can't enjoy myself. That I can't enjoy being here with all of you." She tried to mean it. She *had* been enjoying it, but there was no escaping the pain, either. Still. Always.

"No worries," Reka said. "You're part of it. No escape. Marry this bad boy, and you're part of us." Her nod was as firm as her voice, and Josie thought she was surely going to cry now.

"I know about that, too, wanting to be part of it," Jenna said. Josie could tell from the look Jenna shot her, the final press of her hand, that she was taking the spotlight off her, and she was grateful.

"I had the opposite thing, you know," she told Josie. "I wasn't sure if...everyone would accept me either, because I was different too. In a different way. I wondered if they'd think that Finn married me just because I was pregnant." She had a couple spots of color on her cheeks now. "True confessions, except it isn't, because everyone here knows it, except maybe you. It's no secret that we didn't have Lily after ten months. We had her after six. And I wasn't sure how that would go over. With anyone. I know it was tough at the school dropoff, because I was Finn's nanny. Guess everyone knows that too. All the mums sure did. When I turned up that first day with the kids, after the holidays, with the ring, and the belly..."

"And with me," Finn put in, his face set in the hard lines that showed exactly how he'd earned his fearsome reputation. "And nobody said a bloody thing, did they?" He looked like he wanted to punch somebody right now, and Josie'd have bet that nobody had *ever* said a thing, not when he was around.

"Not to you," Jenna said, echoing Josie's thoughts. "And not to my face. But I knew what they were saying behind my back. And I was so afraid that all of you would be saying the same thing," she told the others. "Since I'd only met any of you as Finn's nanny. That first barbecue, at your house," she told Drew, "that was rough."

"Nah," he said with the gentle smile that had come as a surprise to Josie. "No worries."

Reka snorted. "Oh, yeh. You should have told me this sooner. I could've set your mind at rest. Think we knew you were more than the nanny a good long time before that."

Jenna looked startled. "You did? But you couldn't have. We didn't even...we weren't even..."

She was redder than ever, and Finn chuckled, his expression having lost the frost. "You're reckoning without Reka's magical powers."

"Such a thing as chemistry," Reka went on, ignoring him. "And we're not blind. So tell us. What did happen, with the wedding and all? All we knew was, Finn was at Koti's wedding alone one month, as usual, and the next thing we knew, Hemi tells me he's turned up at training the next month with a shiny ring on and his mouth shut, again as usual. Or else Hemi just didn't ask," she said with a reproving glance at her husband, who was laughing now. "All I got was that Finn was married, and who he'd married, which wasn't exactly an earthshaking surprise, like I said. But seems Hemi didn't bother to get any more info than that. I didn't know about the baby until you turned up at that first game."

"Imagine depriving you like that," Hemi said with a shake of the head. "All that time wasted, when you didn't know the whole story. What was I thinking? I know you'll be shocked to learn this, but we don't actually sit around the gym and open our hearts to each other. I didn't know because Finn didn't tell me."

"Really?" Jenna looked at Finn, who was smiling now along with the rest of the men. "You didn't tell them?"

"Of course I didn't tell them," he said in exasperation. "Not their business, was it. It was your story to tell or not, anyway, not mine."

"Well, since Finn deprived us then," Reka urged, "tell us now."

finn gets his way

♡

Jenna looked around. It felt...bare, to share this with them. But look at what Josie had shared. There were no real secrets here. They all knew she'd been the nanny, and unless their math skills were seriously deficient, they all knew when she'd got pregnant.

"When we got...engaged, I guess you'd call it," she said slowly, "we were in Motueka, near Finn's family. And we didn't have anything. Any friends around. Anybody but his family. Any plan, any way to do it. I mean..." She looked at Finn for help.

"Any clothes," he put in helpfully. "No clothes to get married in. And Jenna didn't have many clothes left at all, by the time I got through with her. And what d'you mean, 'I guess you'd call it?' I did my best. Got down on a knee and all. I did the business."

She laughed, even though she was embarrassed, and everybody else lost the slightly shocked expression and laughed along with her. "Except that you were down there already. And it wasn't...like that," she explained, flustered, because, well, it *had* been a bit like that. "With the clothes, I mean. It's just that it was all a bit of a surprise."

Finn snorted. "Yeh. You could put it like that."

"I'd call it a surprise and then some," Finn went on, and Jenna sat back, listened to him tell the story, and remembered.

His sister Sarah had brought Harry and Sophie back to the little holiday park office that Christmas day, nearly three years ago now, after Finn had made his unconventional proposal, and Jenna, to her own shock, had accepted him. There'd been some tearful hugging and kissing, and Finn had contributed his fair share of the tears, because Finn was like that.

"So that's all good," Sarah had said with satisfaction after everyone's tears had been dried, everybody was happy again, and the kids were getting busy with their ice blocks. She went to the door and flipped the sign from "Closed" to "Open." "Finally, and it's all happened just because I'm so good. So what's the plan now?"

Jenna looked helplessly at Finn. "I don't know. I can't just leave Sarah. Not at Christmas, with nobody else to help here."

"Bugger that," Finn said roundly. "You're going to leave her. She'll manage."

Jenna was laughing, and crying a little again too, because she couldn't help it. She'd been so tired, and so sick, and so sad for so long, and the sudden change was almost too much to take. "I *can't* just leave you," she told Sarah. "Not when you've been so kind. Not right before Boxing Day, the moment it gets busy."

"Too right you can," Sarah said. "And you're going to. Think this is the first time Kieran and I have been left to shift for ourselves? And here it is for a happy reason, not because some flaky backpacker met a fella she fancied and did a runner. I'm sacking you now. Right now. This minute. The kids are going to help me in here for a bit, and Finn's going to help you pack up your things, and I'm going to ring that girl who was in asking about a job the other day and tell her she's got one. So go on, get out of here, because you're sacked, and I need my cabin back today." She was trying to glare, but it wasn't coming off too well.

"And then we can go to the beach," Harry said happily, his mouth stained red from the ice block he'd just finished. "And Jenna can come! We can show you our swimming! You can do a lesson!"

There had been no arguing, not with Finn's considerable authority backed up by his equally determined sister, not with Jenna's own willful heart overriding every responsible scruple. Ten minutes later, she was in the tiny staff cabin she shared with a German girl, emptying her possessions into her single suitcase. And Finn was eyeing her few items of clothing with disgust.

"Thought you'd given up wearing things that are too big for you," he said, holding out a pair of baggy green shorts that earned themselves a withering frown.

She grabbed for them, tugged when he held on, and had to laugh. "Finn. Give them to me. I won't have anything to wear. I had to get rid of a lot of things, because nothing fit, and I didn't have a lot of money to shop. I had to take what I could get."

He yanked the shorts out of her grasp and stuffed them firmly into the rubbish. "That's it. We're leaving the kids here, flying to Auckland tomorrow, and doing some shopping. I've got something I need to buy there anyway, a ring I've got to put on somebody, and I'm not having my wife looking like she got dressed out of the rag bin."

My wife. She stopped packing, and he saw the expression on her face. His own face softened, and he pulled her into his arms.

"I like the sound of that," he told her. "Hope you do too, because we're getting married inside a week, I promise you that. I've learned my lesson. I'm not letting you go again."

"Yes," she said, hiding her face against his shoulder so the words came out muffled. "I like it. I do."

"Crying again, eh." He cuddled her a bit more, stood back a pace, laid one big hand across her belly, felt the swelling there, so distinct now.

"I want to see you show this off," he told her gently. "I want to buy you some better clothes so you can do it properly, so you can feel pretty. Because you've been hiding it, haven't you?"

She wiped her eyes and nodded, unable to say more. She didn't have to anyway, because he knew, and he knew what it had cost her to do it.

"Then let's get this done," he said, "because I want to take you swimming in those pretty togs of yours, see this little belly we made."

She laughed through the tears that still flowed, because the feeling of him touching the place where their baby grew was so precious. Something she'd never, ever thought she'd get to feel.

"I don't have that one anymore, though," she told him. "Your favorite. I've bought that other one instead, the one you wanted at the beginning. The navy-blue one with the little skirt."

"No." He looked truly horrified, and she had to laugh again.

"It was the only one in the shop that fit." She cupped a breast, more generous than ever now, and if she was teasing him a little, well, she was entitled. "I'm hard to fit. Especially now."

He was smiling, and then he wasn't. Finn had never been slow on the uptake. His reaction time was legendary, and right now, he was reacting to her. Before she could do more than blink, he had her hauled up against him with one big arm, had the other hand behind her head, and was kissing her like he meant it.

That was fine with her, because she meant it too. Her body was responding to him in the same way it always had. More, because every single one of her hormones seemed to be springing to life and demanding that he touch her body. Right now. Everywhere.

She'd tried to forget this. She'd tried so hard. And she hadn't even come close.

"I want to be romantic," he groaned against her mouth, "but could we take that as read? Because I need to touch you. I haven't made love to you since…"

"October thirtieth," she said with a gasp as his mouth reached her throat, at the faint scratch of whiskers against her skin, because Finn's beard grew so fast. At the feel of him, the size of his shoulders, the breadth of his back under her palms. The strength and bulk of him so comforting, and so thrilling at the same time. "But…ah… who's counting."

He was pulling her onto the narrow bottom bunk with him, ducking to fit. "I love you. I do. But I need to be inside you."

She couldn't answer, because she was too busy pulling his shirt up over his head, shoving him down on the bed, running her palms over the light furring of hair on his chest, sinking her teeth into the heavy muscle of his shoulder and hearing his indrawn breath, his start of surprise.

She bit again, excitement at what she was doing mixing with the thrumming of nerve endings everyplace he was touching her. He was reaching for her too, his hand diving inside the neckline of her dress to cup a breast, stroke her there, needing to hold her as much as she needed to touch him.

"Hungry?" he asked, his voice coming out a little strangled at the feel of her teeth on his skin. "Or just... ah...taking it out on me?"

She didn't answer right away, just rolled so she was on top of him, bit him hard again, then kissed the spot, taking satisfaction in seeing the faint red mark her teeth had left. Up the bulky line of shoulder to the broad column of his throat, and she had to bite him there too.

He tasted like salt and man. He tasted like Finn, and all she wanted was to explore that big body with her hands and her eager mouth.

"Both," she told him. If he needed her, she needed him just as much. "Hungry for you, and taking it out on you too. I'm going to take it all out on you. I'm going to make you sorry."

She could feel what her words did to him, and she smiled in satisfaction, did some more biting, could feel from the strain against her how hard he was working to hold himself back, how much he wanted it.

She had his clothes off before he did hers, did as much touching and kissing as the tiny space allowed before he caught up, and, finally, overtook her, exactly as she'd known he would. Before he'd rolled her again, had wrestled her clothes off with a few choice words, and had reminded her of what she'd been missing.

The bed was much too small for him, and by the time they'd finished, he'd banged his head on the upper bunk, his elbow against the wall, his foot against the post. And none of it seemed to matter to him one bit.

They did the best they could, and if he swore from time to time along the way, it was nothing to what came out of his mouth when he was over her, sliding into her, moving in her, going so deep, and still taking care not to be too rough. Taking too much care, until, at last, she wrapped her arms and legs around him and urged him on, because she needed more.

"Harder," she gasped. "Finn. Harder. Please. Do it hard."

"Don't want to…hurt you," he managed, and she could feel the restraint, the tension in the shoulders she was gripping with all her might.

She ran her hands down the length of his spine, back up again, faster and faster, then slid them down to the powerful buttocks, took one in each hand, and tried to force what she needed from him. "I need it harder," she told him fiercely. "Do it."

He growled. Actually growled. Deep and rough, and she got what she wanted. Everything she wanted. All of him, no holds barred. All the way.

It was a squeeze, when he had rolled off of her again. Finn in a narrow twin bunk bed didn't leave much room for her at all. Which meant they had to snuggle.

He got his breath back, laughed a little.

"What?" she asked, trailing her hand down his side, touching his big body just because she wanted to. "I'm funny?"

"Nah. Even though you are. Who knew my sweet, sexy nanny would turn out to be so...demanding? I'm going to make you kiss every one of those marks you made. So you know. Something to think about while we have that swim. Before I take you to bed again tonight and show you exactly how much I've been missing you, once I have room to..." He smiled. "Express myself. But nah. I was laughing because I was just thinking—so much better without the condom. Hell of a way to get to feel you like that. And there I was, being so careful all that time, when I could've had all that. Just as well, because I'd never have let you out of bed."

"It really feels that much better?" Her hand was still stroking his shoulder, exploring everyplace she could touch, because she couldn't stand not to do it.

"Oh, yeh," he assured her. "Feels so good, I'm going to have to have it again just to make sure. As soon as possible. Tonight."

He gave her a final lingering kiss, ran his hand over her as dust motes danced in a shaft of sunlight that fell in a bar across her body, a diagonal stripe over her full white breast, her rapidly disappearing waistline. He followed that line of sunshine with his hand, and she shifted a little under the caress of warm sun and warmer hand. Big and hard, just like all of him. All except his deceptively soft heart.

How she'd missed that hand, that heart. She'd never thought she'd feel his touch again, and her eyes filled with tears once more at having him back, at knowing she could keep him. That he was here, and this was real.

"What, the thought of being in my bed that bad?" he teased gently, his hand going up to wipe away the treacherous moisture that spilled down her cheek. "If I'm not doing it right anymore, you don't have to cry. All you have to do is tell me what you want, and you know I'll try harder for you." He smiled down at her, gave her a kiss on the forehead.

She laughed, though it came out a little shaky. "Yeah. I definitely think you should try harder. Because you didn't satisfy me nearly enough. Maybe after two or three more times, though, it might get tolerable again. Though you may need to do it a different way next time. You know, keep me from getting bored."

His deep chuckle was her answer. "You know I'll be doing it some different ways. Soon as we've got a bed I can move in. But come on." He gave her a gentle slap on the bum. "Rattle your dags. Sarah's going to think we've eloped right now."

"Oh," Jenna said with a smile of her own, "I think Sarah's going to have a pretty good idea of why packing took us so long."

He laughed again. "You could be right at that. And we don't even have to hide anymore. Though I'll admit that sneaking around had its moments. Come on. I'll help you pack your things."

And he did. Well, if "help" meant "throw most of them away," because that was what he did.

He was especially caustic about her underwear. "Thought we were done with this industrial-strength stuff," he complained, holding up a white bra that wasn't going to be featuring in anybody's fantasies, a sturdy pair of white cotton briefs. One dangling from each hand, until he tossed them with decision into the rubbish bin that already held most of the rest of her wardrobe.

"All you need is something to wear for about, oh, twenty-four hours," he promised at her protest. "Because after that, like I said. Shopping."

"So I still don't understand," Reka said when Finn had finished telling the story. Leaving out all the best parts, luckily. "You didn't have clothes."

"Yeah," Jenna said. "Because I was...well, no surprise. I was pretty pregnant. And Finn didn't think I was... well-dressed."

That got a snort from him. "Could say that, yeh. Or you could say that I tossed everything you had into the rubbish. Would've burnt it, but, you know. Time. Priorities."

Jenna was laughing. "He did. He really did. So we left the kids with his folks, flew back to Auckland, and... bought things. I got so worn out, in the end," she confessed, "that by the time we were buying the ring..."

"She cried," Finn put in helpfully. "Too tired, too hungry. Had to take her to a café for a rest and a nibble, go finish the job myself. Ever hear of a woman who couldn't handle buying her own jewelry?"

"It made it better, though," Jenna said, "having you bring the ring back to me and show me." She ran a thumb over the big square-cut emerald, outlined with tiny diamonds, that sat on her ring finger. "To see what you chose for me, and have you tell me why you picked it. It made it romantic."

Finn was looking at her, his mouth open in outrage again, and she was laughing, and so was everybody else. "Not that it wasn't anyway," she told him soothingly. "It was all very romantic. It was beautiful. And then you took me to the pub for dinner, and that was wonderful too."

"Aw, nice," Koti grinned. "Took her to the pub and all. You're a regular Sir Galahad, aren't you. You're just chokka with romance. What'd you do after the wedding, I wonder? Take her to Maccas for a burger? Buy her an extra Fluffy all her own?"

"No," Jenna was laughing harder now, her hands over her belly. "Because it was in his parents' back garden. All of us, and his…" She hiccupped with it. "Family. And no…McDonalds in Motueka. We had leftover Christmas ham. His mum defrosted it. And it was…"

She sat up, wiped her streaming eyes with the backs of her hands, choked back one final bubble of hilarity, then reached up, gave Finn a quick kiss, laid a hand on the side of his face, and smiled into his eyes. Saw him trying to look stern, the smile that couldn't help escaping all the same, and loved him so much.

She said the final words to him. For him. Let him know what she felt, and knew that he knew. That it was all right, and it always would be. "And it was beautiful," she said. "It was perfect."

pak 'n' save

♡

"Aren't we stopping at Pak 'n' Save?" Hannah asked in surprise.

They'd finally left the beach, because the kids needed naps. She'd known how much Drew was enjoying this relaxed time, so rare in his busy life. He needed the chance to catch up with his old mates, and she hadn't wanted to break up the party, even though she'd have been more than ready to leave an hour earlier.

Now Drew had failed to indicate for the turn, and she sighed. "I thought we needed ice."

Drew shot her a glance across the car. "Thought I'd come back for it once we've got the kids down. And you too."

"I'm not that fragile." She heard the tension in her voice, took a breath. "We're here. It'll take fifteen minutes, and forty-five by the time you make a separate trip. We need a few other things anyway. Too many people in the house."

Another look, but he turned without a word at the next corner, began the series of quick lefts that would take him back to the supermarket. "Thought it might be too much for you," he finally said. "We could've had Mako and Kristen stay at the hotel with the others. Still can, for that matter. You don't have to say it, if that's what you're worried about. I will."

"I don't mind." She shifted her position and sighed again.

"Back aching?" he asked, seeing it.

"A bit. Never mind. No, I want them with us, you know I do. And your parents too. It'd be pretty ungrateful of me to say anything else, wouldn't it? Your mum's doing practically all my cooking and laundry for me. Taking care of my kids, too, when you don't."

"Thought they were *our* kids."

"You're right. I mean, of course they are." How was this going so wrong? Every word was spiky, weighted, and all she'd wanted to do was agree, get along. "I'm sorry." She heard the miserable apology, tried to inject some lightness into her tone. "Don't pay any attention to me. It's fifteen minutes. I'm good if you are. Pregnant wife, sandy kids. Pak 'n' Save. Ice and bread and milk. Sir Andrew Callahan, hero of the nation, welcome to your life."

♡

He decided to ignore the fact that she was trying to jolly him, as if he were the one who needed it.

"Right." He pulled into the carpark, busy with arriving and departing cars on a Sunday afternoon in December, shoppers in and out of the sliding glass doors, shorts and jandals and sun hats and a holiday mood. He thought about suggesting she wait in the car for him and the kids, decided against it. He got out of the car, pulled Grace out of her car seat and hoisted her in an arm, grabbed hold of Jack's hand.

"Can we have ice cream, Mum?" Jack asked, skipping along beside him but looking, as always, to his mother.

Which was what Drew got for all those late-night planning sessions, just as Finn had said.

Well, it was his job. Nothing to be done about that. He always had breakfast with them, anyway, when he was home. That one was inviolable. When he was home.

"No ice cream," Drew answered for her. "You had your lunch, and your granny will be giving you your tea at home soon enough. No room in that belly for ice cream."

"I've got room," Jack insisted. "I'm *empty*. I *need* ice cream." And despite himself, Drew had to smile.

"Ice cream!" Grace echoed happily, bang on time.

Drew ignored the suggestion, gave her a kiss on top of her blonde curls, and followed his wife into the refrigerated cool of the cavernous supermarket, wishing he felt better about how she was walking.

"Bread, milk, eggs, right?" he asked, sliding Grace into the front carrier seat of the trolley that Hannah had pulled out as Jack ran to hop on the end for a ride. "Anything else we need, besides the ice?"

"Tea," Hannah said. "I'll get that, if you grab the rest."

It was more like five minutes, after all. Not too bad.

"Come on, mate," he told Jack, leaving the trolley with Hannah to push through the checkout. "We'll go get the ice for your mum, because that's a man job." He winked at Hannah, who smiled back at him. Doing her best, like always.

He pulled two heavy bags from the bin near the doors, turned to find that Jack had run to the ice cream freezer despite everything he'd told him, was standing on the edge, trying to hoist himself up on his sturdy legs to peer inside.

"Let's go," he told his son.

"Ice cream's here, Dad," Jack insisted. "It's in here."

"I know it is," Drew said. He shoved one bag under an arm, ignoring the freezing cold against his body, transferred the other bag so he had a hand free, and reached for Jack's. "But we're going."

"I *want* it," Jack insisted, clinging to the freezer like a limpet. "I'm *empty!*"

This time, Drew didn't smile. "No," he said flatly. "Your mum's tired, and so's your sister. They both need a nap. And so do you," he added recklessly, knowing how much Jack hated to be reminded of nap time and not caring one bit. He'd placate his wife any day of the week. Damned if he was going to placate his four-year-old son.

Jack clung obstinately to the side of the freezer, and Drew didn't have enough hands to pry him loose, didn't want to risk hurting him by yanking him off. "I don't need a nap!" Jack insisted. "I'm not a baby. And why does Mum need a nap? Mum's not a baby either."

"No, she's not a baby. She's a tired woman," Drew snapped.

Entire newspaper columns had been written about his legendary patience. Patient and controlled, that was Drew Callahan. Always had been.

Well, he wasn't feeling patient now. One four-year-old boy, it was clear, had more power to test him than the dirtiest-playing opponent, the most incompetent ref known to world rugby. "She's about to have a baby," he told Jack, "and pregnant women get tired. Which means my job right now, and yours too, is to help her."

"Why does she have to have a baby?" Jack demanded, not letting go of his beloved freezer. "She *has* a baby. She has Gracie. She doesn't need another baby. If she didn't have a baby, she wouldn't be tired, and I could have ice cream. I don't think she should have one."

"You don't get a vote." Drew bit the words out. "And this discussion is over. We are taking this ice to your mum. We are paying. We are going home. And everyone is having a nap. Now."

His son looked at him, his expression mulish, the very salt-stiffened tufts of brown hair sticking up from his head exuding defiance. He'd come down from the freezer case at last, was all but stomping in his little blue jandals. "I don't *want* to," he said. "I don't want a nap, and I don't want a baby brother! You keep saying it's nice, but it *isn't*. It *isn't* nice, and I don't *want* it!" He started to cry, and that was just wonderful. That took the cake. "I want *ice cream!*"

"Right." Drew squatted, still holding his ice, the entire side of his body numb with cold by now, and grabbed Jack under the bum. He slung him over one big shoulder, edged his way around the queue of shoppers, dumped the bags into Hannah's trolley without a word, and carried his kicking, screaming son out of the store, knowing that everyone there was watching him go. He'd had better moments.

When Hannah pushed the trolley out to the car, Drew was crouched down next to it, one hand on Jack's shoulder, having what was clearly a man-to-man talk.

He stood at her approach. "One sec." He opened the door for Jack, made sure he was buckled into his booster seat. Her son was still sobbing a bit, and Hannah couldn't bring herself to care. Drew was right, he was *their* son, not just hers. Drew was going to have to handle this, because she couldn't. Not right now.

She was about to lift Grace out of the trolley, but Drew was there again. "What are you thinking?" he asked her, the impatience evident. "Lifting ten kilos? No."

"Eleven," she said automatically. "And who do you think has been lifting her all this time?"

He sighed. "Get in the car."

She didn't argue, just climbed in and leaned her head against the passenger seat. She heard him buckling Gracie in behind her, talking to her a bit, jollying her, because one grizzling child was enough. He unloaded the trolley into the boot, was back in a minute, climbing into the car and turning the key, the air conditioning coming to life along with the engine, providing blessed relief from the summer heat.

He looked across at her, smiled a little. "Here's where you tell me I was right. Should have let me come back for the groceries."

She tried to laugh, but her eyes filled with tears all the same. "Sorry. You were right. I didn't realize how...close to the edge we all were. Thought we could squeeze in one more thing. Sorry."

"Aw, sweetheart." He put a hand behind her neck, gave it a bit of a rub. "No worries. Bath, nap. Good as gold."

She laughed a little shakily. "Who are you talking to? Jack or me? I know I'm acting four myself."

"Nah." He backed out of the space, indicated left out of the carpark, and headed for home. "Just too pregnant. Most women in your shape wouldn't be having house guests. Or a dinner party."

♡

"Righty-o, then," he said as they set the groceries onto the kitchen bench, Helen following behind with Grace. "Go on up. Mum and I've got this."

"The kids…" Her feet were lead, and her body wasn't much better. All she wanted was to lie down and sleep for about fifteen hours. "They need a bath first."

"Got it," he repeated. "Go. Bath. Nap. Now."

"Bossy," she said with a sigh and a smile she couldn't help.

"Yeh. Tell me about it later. Go."

madam

♡

Hannah woke two hours later to the sound of Drew moving quietly around the bedroom, opening drawers. Changing, she realized fuzzily.

"Hey," she said with a sleepy smile.

"Hey." He came and sat beside her on the bed, helped her haul herself up against the pillows. He saw the ripple of movement under the tight white T-shirt, put a hand on the low, round bulge of her belly. "Whoa. Having a party in there."

"Feels like he's doing the haka." She shifted a bit on the bed to get more comfortable, then put her hand over his, moving it. "That's a foot. Feel that?"

"Strong, too," he said. "This one's a kicker, eh. You growing me another All Black in there? If he's a back, Hemi'll never let me hear the end of it."

She smiled. "You never know. He'll come out as who he is, we both know that. And who he is, is active. Only naps when I'm walking around carrying him, just like Jack. Hope that's not an omen. At least Gracie's a good sleeper."

He frowned a bit. "Yeh. When all three of them are here, and I'm back to work...We're going to talk about that."

"Sounds ominous."

"Nah. Never ominous." His hand left her belly, came up to stroke her cheek, her hair, and she leaned into the thumb cradling her face, because it felt so good. He hadn't put his shirt on yet, and she laid her own hand against his chest just to feel the slab of muscle under her palm.

"Finn may have worked you out too hard this morning," she told him. "But what I didn't tell you is, he did that for me. Our secret."

"Feels good," he said, smiling down at her.

"Yeah," she said, "it does," and smiled back.

He bent down, gave her a long, sweet kiss, fingered the heavy braid that hung over one shoulder. "Pity we've got all these people coming by again. I could use a bit of a reminder right about now that we're not just Mum and Dad. Bet you could too."

She hummed her agreement. "I look like a mum, no getting away from that. But you don't look much like a dad to me." Her fingers traced the white lines of old scars from a shoulder surgery or two. "What you look like is a really hot rugby player. And I hate to tell you, but I've always had this fantasy about a rugby player. I'd share it with you, but it's too embarrassing. I'd blush. And I know you don't want to watch me blush. All over."

She saw his eyes begin to gleam, shivered a little with sleepy pleasure. It was so exciting to tease him a little, even if they weren't being serious.

"Now you know why I insisted on the nap," he said. "Ulterior motive all the way. I'd love to hear about that fantasy later on tonight. Maybe I could pretend to be that rugby player you want so badly. You may want to give it a bit more thought, eh."

He got up with obvious reluctance, went to the closet and pulled a black collared knit shirt off a hanger, tugged it over his broad chest. She watched him cover his body and was sorry to lose the sight, because that muscular torso, the heavy bulk of it, the vee where it narrowed to his waist…He hadn't lost a thing, and it all still worked for her. Boy, did it ever. He was good with clothes on. He was better naked.

"Mmm." She smiled across the dim room at him. He'd closed the blinds while she'd been sleeping, she realized. She'd been too tired to care. "They do say that couples who share their fantasies have better sex. What do you think? Not sure what I could pretend to be at this point, but maybe if you close your eyes…"

"I don't need any fantasy woman," he said. "Already got her."

"Now, I *know* that's not true," she laughed. "Not possible. It's funny, though, isn't it?"

He'd opened his mouth as if he wanted to say something else, but all he said was, "What is?"

"When you were carrying Jack out today, and I was in the queue in my sandy maternity dress, with my sticky baby in the trolley, there was Josie looking back at me from the cover of *Woman's World*. With Hugh, at that TV awards show last month, both of them looking so glamorous. Feeling not one bit glamorous myself, being a little envious, thinking that would be nice. And then catching myself, because how many times has that been us? And now I've met her. Just as sandy as me. If a lot more glamorous, still," she admitted, "because she sure is beautiful, isn't she? But it was pretty funny."

"Never feels the same on the inside as it looks on the outside," he agreed, coming back to sit beside her again, even though they had guests coming in minutes, and he had to get downstairs, and she had to get *up*. "Ever."

"Although Hugh's the only one of you guys who did it right," she said. "The only one marrying a star."

"He's not marrying her because she's a star," Drew said with certainty. "He's marrying a nice Kiwi girl from Katikati. Just like she's not marrying an All Black. That's obvious. Just like you didn't marry me for that."

"Oh, yeah?" She smiled, put her hand on his sizeable thigh this time, beneath the hem of his khaki shorts, and traced the delineated line of quadriceps, the rasp of hair providing the friction she loved. "You sure about that?"

"Dead sure." His own smile reached all the way to his eyes. "You're not that good at pretending."

She laughed. "You're right about that. Pretty sure I married you partly for your outsized Y chromosome, though."

"The missing link, eh." He sighed. "The truth comes out."

He paused, looked thoughtful, not seeming in any hurry to get up, and she kept her hand on his leg, because she always felt better when she was touching him, and waited.

"Whenever I look at those magazines myself, the ones in the supermarket..." he said slowly, and stopped again.

This was rare, Drew sharing, so she hitched herself up a bit to listen harder.

"Well, you and I know it's not really that way, is it?" he continued after a moment. "Even when they're showing something good, that you're meant to want. It's not life. It's one night of...performing for the camera. And how often are they *not* showing something good? Most of the time, seems to me. How often is it some sad Hollywood story about some poor couple breaking up? And you know the story behind it's uglier even than what you'll hear. Broken hearts all over the shop. Not one bit glamorous. Nothing anybody'd want."

"Like Josie's cover," Hannah remembered. "'Our Josie—Happy at Last.' People like to hear about stars, but sometimes I think they like to hear most that stardom doesn't make you happy. So they can feel better about their own lives. They should have got a picture of you carrying Jack out. That'd do it."

He laughed. "Proud parental moment, eh. Bet somebody did get a snap of that. But you know, glamour's never what I wanted. I wanted..."

"What?" she asked, trying to show him how much she wanted to hear.

"My grandfather died when I was twenty-three," he said unexpectedly. "After a couple years of my granny nursing him. Cancer. They were married forty-nine years, I ever tell you that?"

"No," she said. "I don't think so."

"Yeh. I was young, like I said, just starting to do really well with the footy."

"Starting?"

"Well, yeh. Starting. Wasn't the skipper yet."

"Oh," she said. "I see. An All Black, but not the captain. Not yet. Just starting. Got it."

"Anyway," he said. "I was all caught up in that. Came back home when we knew it'd be soon, sitting there by his bed with the others. He died at home, right there with her beside him in her chair. Him looking at her like nobody else was there."

Drew wasn't looking at Hannah now himself, though. His gaze was off in the distance, back to the past. "He looked at her," he said again, "there at the end. Said, 'Hate to leave you alone, Madam. But I'll see you again. No rush. I'll wait. You take your time.'"

"Madam?" she asked through the lump in her throat that had formed at his words. At the heart that had been able to take them in at twenty-three, had held them all this time. Had known how much they mattered.

Drew smiled, remembering. "He always called her that. Funny, eh. I asked him once. He wasn't any kind of flash. A farmer, and she was a farmer's wife. So it seemed... funny. He told me, though. Didn't seem to mind telling me, and he wasn't soft, either. Not a bit. He said it was to remind himself that he was lucky, and to remind her that she was special, when either of them forgot. He'd started out with it as a bit of a joke, when they *were* starting out, but then...it fit, he said. It fit."

"That's a nice story," she said quietly.

He shook his head. "Mum and Dad thought afterwards that now she could have a bit of a rest, maybe even...enjoy herself a little. Once she didn't have to take care of him, you know. Spend some time with her friends. But she didn't even last a year. Heart packed up, the doctor said, and I reckon that's right, but not the way he thought. She didn't complain, always cheerful enough. But I reckon she just didn't want to be in the world without him. Not after all that time. Felt like half of her was missing, she told me once. In a...moment we had."

He looked at her again. "And you know what I thought, when she said that?"

"No," she said, her mouth a little dry, her own heart beating a little hard. "What?"

"I thought, that's what I want. Not then, of course," he said with a little laugh. "I wasn't that noble. But someday.

I knew that was what I wanted someday. I thought, I want a girl I feel that lucky to have. I want a woman I'll want to call Madam when we're seventy, because I'll still feel lucky to have her. Not because she's flash. Not because she's beautiful. But because she's real. Because she's mine."

"In her crumpled sundress, nine months pregnant and grouchy," Hannah said, the tears that were never too far from the surface at war with her smile.

"Yeh," he said. "That woman. That's the one I want. The one in the crumpled sundress. Nine months pregnant and doing her best."

He leaned over, kissed her gently once more. "And for the record?" he told her, stroking a hand over her hair. "She's still beautiful."

something of my own

♡

She came downstairs at last. A bit late, but Drew had urged her not to hurry.

She could see through the open ranch sliders from the dining room that Koti, Liam, and Hemi were already out there, washing down tables and chairs on the grass with Jack and Gracie's questionable help while Drew started the barbecue and his mum and Kristen relaxed in chairs on the patio.

Our kids, she reminded herself, resisting the urge to check on them, to ask Helen about their tea, to worry about them. Drew was out there. Helen was out there. Hannah didn't need to be out there. Not tonight.

Reka and Kate were busy in the kitchen as well, Reka making room in the fridge for the container of marinated chicken pieces, the plate of mince already pressed into burgers, while Kate hauled vegies out of a bag.

"Jenna's coming soon," Reka informed Hannah. "She was over at my place earlier, helping me fix all this, making the sweets as well. She and Finn are just getting Harry settled at Nic's parents'. He's spending the night with Zack. Sleepover. We've got the other two at our place with Mum."

"And Maia," Kate said. "Your mum's a saint, Reka."

Reka laughed. "Nah. You know better than that. A Maori mum with the mokopuna? She'll be enjoying it. And she's got those two little madams to help her. Nothing Ariana and Sophie love more than being told they're in charge."

"That's true," Hannah said. "Oldest-child syndrome. I was a bit that way myself. Kristen would tell you so, I'm sure. But what can I do?" She saw the chilly bins out on the patio. Drew had put his ice to good use already, it seemed. Everything seemed pretty well under control, in fact.

"Sit," Reka said. "Keep us company."

"I could slice vegetables," Hannah said.

"Or you could sit," Reka said. "You're contributing your house, and that's the only thing in the world that you and Kristen need to do tonight. That and chat, of course. Once you're past eight months, you get a pass." She pulled out a chair and all but pushed Hannah into it.

"I seem to recall you making me dinner once or twice when you were about eight months along yourself," Hannah said.

"Because I wanted to. And as soon as I didn't want to and my mum was there, I relaxed, so I'd have a bit of energy left once the baby showed up."

"You tell her, Reka," Kate said, pulling out the cutting board, because of course she knew where it was, as many times as she'd visited over the couple years since Hannah and Drew had moved to Tauranga. "Besides, this is my one and only job. I know you're better than me at everything, Hannah, but just for tonight, could we pretend it isn't true and let me help? I was going to do more, but Reka said she and Jenna would do it, and I should just wait for them to give me jobs." She sighed. "Probably best. I'm a much better accountant than I am a cook. Koti's definitely gotten better, but I still lag horribly. I hate to admit that he made our contribution tonight."

She was left with nothing to do but answer the door, and do some chatting. An hour later, the kids had been taken off for their own tea and bedtime by Sam and Helen, and Hannah and Drew were sitting with seven couples around those cleaned tables. The sun was still strong in the warm summer evening, making her grateful for the vine-covered pergola shading the patio of irregular, cream-colored flagstones.

It was all serenity here, the expanse of grass beyond the warm stones mowed just that morning by Sam, the border beyond made up of native plantings, flax and fern, palms both tall and short. No view of the sea back here, of course, but the privacy Drew needed. The place where he could relax, because anyone who got this far was a friend.

Just like everybody who was sitting around the tables tonight. Everyone had come except Josie and Hugh, because they were having dinner with Josie's family. Only two nights to go until the wedding, and Hannah thought she knew how Josie was feeling. A husband, and two kids as well. A lot to take on. But it seemed like the two kids were a bonus, and Hannah was glad of that for all their sakes.

Koti was talking to her, and she brought her thoughts back to the present.

"Potato salad," he said proudly, holding the heavy glass bowl for Hannah so she could help herself. "This is mine. You need to have some, because it's what Americans eat at a barbecue. Kate's mum taught me to make it when we were over there visiting with the baby last year. I just about fell asleep during the baseball game her dad took me to, and I can't make a cherry pie like George Washington, but I can do this, and corn on the cob on the barbie. I can eat watermelon and spit the seeds, too. Even sang along with the national anthem. Reckon that makes me a Yank, or at least half of one, just like Maia."

"Oh, yeah," Kate said. "You blended right in. Must have been the tattoo. Didn't stand out at all. None of my old friends was scooting her chair a little closer just to get a better look and hear your cute accent, for instance. And by the way, George Washington chopped down the cherry tree, he didn't make a cherry *pie.*"

He just grinned. "Knew it was something to do with cherries. Though why that'd be something heroic to celebrate, I'm buggered if I know."

I'll tell you the fascinating story later," Kate promised. "So you can pass it along to your child someday. As the half-Yank you are."

"Not a true story, actually," Jenna said, laughing. "So Koti could skip it, if he likes."

"No, really?" Koti said. "Well, that's a relief."

"It was in a book for children," Jenna explained, "around the turn of the nineteenth century. A biography, but mostly made up, I'm afraid, and it ended up as one of those things that got passed down ever since. I guess the intention was a good one. That particular story is about not lying."

"It isn't true?" Emma asked. "I never knew that."

"Jenna knows many things," Finn said. "If it's about teaching and kids, she knows it."

"Are you planning to go back to teaching soon, Jenna?" Hannah asked.

"No," she said, still smiling. "Not for a while yet."

"About five or six years plus two months of a while," Finn put in, putting a proprietary hand on the significant bulge of her abdomen. "Minimum, because I take a fair bit of looking after. And oh, yeh. Four kids. That."

"Four," Hannah said with a sigh. "I'll admit, I'm a bit worried about three."

"Ah. Perfect opening," Drew said. "What kind of help d'you have with that, Jenna?"

"Plenty of house cleaning," she said. "And a fair bit of minding the kids as well, when I need it. Because you can't take three with you to the doctor, and four..." She shuddered. "I hate to imagine. And even though Finn isn't gone as much now, he's gone enough."

"Don't need to justify that to me," Reka said. "That's why my mum lives with us, isn't it. And why Josie's auntie and uncle have moved into her old place, for that matter. To look after the kids when he's gone and she's working."

"And you don't ever feel..." Hannah asked hesitantly. She wasn't sure how to ask this without insulting Reka or Jenna.

Reka looked around the table. "Who here's got some help at home? Family, or somebody else? Everybody, that's who," she told Hannah. "Everybody with kids. I know what you're saying. And no. I don't. I'm a good mum."

"I know you are," Hannah hastened to say. She could feel herself flushing. "I wasn't meaning it was bad to have help. Not for anybody here. I have help myself. How could I say that?" She tried to think of what she could add. How many times did that make it that she'd messed up today?

"Just not enough help," Drew said, clearly not aware that any fence needed mending. "Not enough at all, with what you have to cope with just now. And not if you want to get back into the work, especially."

"That's true," Emma told her earnestly. "There's no way I could work for 2nd Hemisphere without it. You of all people know that, Hannah, even the half-time I do it. And I want to work. I know I could have taken this whole year off, since George, but I didn't want to. I finally got the chance to do something I love doing, and I want to *do* it."

"Me too," Kate said. "That's why we've got a nanny ourselves, so I can. Why we haven't started that second baby yet, too, tell you the truth. Nothing to do with Koti's, um…"

"Aw, nice," he groaned as everyone started to laugh. "Koti's um? Koti's what? Impotence? Low sperm count?"

"Well, *you* know," she flashed back. "In case they were wondering. I'm just saying it's me, not you."

"Trust me," he said, scowling around the table. "Nobody's wondering."

"Oh, I don't know," Nic said. "I know I am. Do tell, Kate."

"Hannah wants to keep up with her own job as well," Drew cut in, his authority, as always, carrying the day. "As much as she can. That's why we're having the conversation. Not to hear about Koti's um."

"See, Kate," Koti said. "*That's* why we're having the conversation. Not for you to cast doubts on my virility."

She sighed. "And men say women are oversensitive. Koti is exceedingly virile," she told the table. "Frighteningly virile. Enormously virile. How's that? Are we all good?"

"Personally, I'm more than good," Nic said. "In fact, I'm repulsed, and more than ready to move on. Suppose Hannah tells us about her work plans, distracts us until we can go home and scrub our brains of some truly disgusting images that I could have gone my entire life without entertaining."

Hannah was laughing. "All Drew's fault. He's the one who brought it up. But all right. I'll do my bit on the distraction, because really, Kate. Eww. I do want to keep working, at least some, as soon as I can again. I don't want to let it all go. I want to be more than the...spokesmodel, or whatever, for my lines."

"Spokesmodel?" Reka asked. "You? I'd say that was us, wouldn't you? Although now that you've got Kristen over here, maybe you can put the rest of us out to pasture. Don't know how she escaped that last shoot for the maternity wear, but surely you can have her holding the new baby in the next one, wearing that nursing top or whatever, making every woman watching feel like she'd better get busy with those press-ups and that ab work."

"No, thanks," Kristen said. She was always quiet in the group, a little shy, but now she spoke up. "I don't model anymore. Hannah knows that."

"Then you're the only one here who can say no to Hannah," Reka said. "Not when she gets that sweet little face and begs you. Drew can't, I know that. And I'd have said Drew could do anything."

"Not that," Drew agreed with a grin, leaning back with one big elbow on the back of Hannah's chair, his thumb stroking over the back of her neck again. "Resist her sweet face? Nah. Can't do that, and she knows it."

"Nobody here has to model if they don't want to," Hannah assured Reka, then had to give Drew a somewhat misty smile. If he'd got up today with a plan to make her feel precious to him, he couldn't have done a much better job. Telling everybody that? That wasn't like him. "Or if they don't want their kids to. Nobody has to do that either. It's only if it's fun. You know that."

"Aw, love," Reka said, "you know we all do know it. Just teasing. Hannah's in fashion, just like Kristen," she explained to Ally, and Hannah should have done that, should have made sure Ally felt included. She wasn't doing well enough at the hostess duties tonight, that was for sure. Good thing Reka was more than capable of taking them on.

"Ally knows," Hannah said, with a belated smile in Ally's direction. "She was Kristen's roommate when they moved here, remember? So we got the chance to get to know her. And this time, we get Nate here too. Another bonus."

Which might have been laying it on a bit thick, but she didn't want anyone to think that she was jealous of Nate's encroachment on Drew's stature. Even though, all right, maybe she was. It had been so hard on Drew to hang up his boots, and if Hannah were forced to tell the truth, it had been hard on her too. And the thought that somebody else could be the captain of the All Blacks…yes, it was definitely still hard.

The first time she and Drew had watched the team run out of the tunnel before the match behind Nate—she hadn't needed to look at Drew to know what a wrench it was. Not that he'd said anything, but the very immobility of his face told the story. The aching desire to be out there at the head of his men, leading them into battle once more. If it could have been done by strength of mind and force of will, he'd have been there that night, and every game since. But a loose forward's body took a battering in rugby, especially one with a workrate like Drew's.

The decision had been his. "If I'm not the best choice for the team," he'd told her before he'd made his announcement, "it's time to take myself out. I'm still the best choice. But barely, and I won't be much longer. I'm not taking that slide."

It had been time. But that didn't make it easy. Then. Still.

"Yes," Ally said, and Hannah wrenched herself back once again. "You and Drew have always been great about inviting me. And I haven't forgotten that you introduced me to Nate in the first place. I wasn't sure that was such a wonderful idea for a while there, but my opinion of him's picked up considerably since then. But sorry," she said, and she was laughing herself, "I'm all distracted."

"Nah, don't apologize," Nate said. "I'm loving thinking that I've got you distracted. You just keep thinking about me."

"A little rude, though," Ally said. "Sorry. Hannah's work. Ahem. No, I hardly know anything about that. Because Kiwis never talk about their work during social time, I found that out pretty fast, and you've obviously picked right up on that, Hannah."

"Yeh, well," Reka said, as aware of the undercurrents as Hannah was, Hannah could tell, and making it clear where her own loyalties lay, "the maternity and kids' wear that 2nd Hemisphere's doing now, those were Hannah's lines. The ones she started for them, her ideas. Of course they jumped at it, because she has the perfect platform for it. They'd have been fools not to. And being the marketing brain she is, didn't take her a minute to think of getting all us WAGs to do some modeling. Which we're not obligated to do," she said pointedly for Hannah's benefit, "but which, astonishingly, we all do anyway. Nothing serious, just a day in the studio with the kids, a video for the website. Everybody loves an All Black, and they even love an All Black's kids. May not want to know that an All Black has a partner, of course, but I don't mind reminding them, especially as it doesn't hurt the team either. Glam up, get the full makeup on, look like an actual WAG for a day. Not to mention remind the female population that these fellas do have partners and kids, just in case that slips their minds. I don't mind doing that, either. I don't mind doing that at all."

Hemi laughed. "Maybe you want to make your point a little clearer, sweetheart. Somebody down in Hawkes Bay may not have got it. I think you were a bit...what was that thing Hugh wasn't? Oh, yeh. Subtle."

"Just as long as you got it," she said.

"Oh, I got it," he assured her. "No worries. I got it a long time ago."

"Why anybody'd want to see the softer side of sports-men at all," Finn put in, "still baffles me, but they seem to all the same. The mums seem to, at least, and the mums are the ones buying the clothes, and it helps Hannah and Emma, so..." He shrugged. "It's all good, far as I'm con-cerned. Jenna always looks pretty. And Sophie likes it all right. Harry, now...he's not too keen. But he does it any-way, every time, when Jenna asks him. A man will do just about any mad thing for the woman he loves, eh."

"So that's it," Hannah told Ally. "That's my other baby, my product lines. They're my ideas, and I love them. And I don't want to just be a name on them. I mean, I want to be able to put *my* name on them, *my* stamp, not just...Drew's name. I want to know that I'm still involved with them, still directing the strategic planning, at least, even though people like Emma are the ones doing the real work, designing the clothes, and others are doing the day-to-day marketing stuff I can't manage anymore. But I need to know for myself, at least, that it's real."

Ally nodded. "Sounds completely reasonable to me."

"It should," Nate said. "Seeing as Ally's got plans to open a gym of her own pretty soon, and I already know Mako and I are going to be putting in some pretty frequent appearances."

"Nate," Ally protested. "I can volunteer *you.* I can assume *you.* I may have to actually *ask* Liam. You don't just get to tell him."

"Nah," Liam said with a grin. "When the skipper asks, it's not a request. That's how it works. Thinking you may be able to get a pretty good turnout for your grand opening, Ally. And not just from the Hurricanes."

"We'll all come," Kate promised. "When is it?"

"Getting way ahead of myself," Ally said, holding up a protesting hand and laughing, but looking so pleased. "I just got my diploma. I mean, just last *week.*"

"And she's got a whole plan already," Nate said proudly. "Going to happen soon enough. Good investment, eh. I tried to invest in my brother's feed business, got told off in no uncertain terms. Good thing I saved my money, because feed and grain, or girls in climbing harnesses?" He sighed with satisfaction. "One of my favorite things to look at, and Ally's got all kinds of plans to attract women to the gym. I can see my presence is going to be required early and often. Observation, supervision, that'll be me."

"Oh, yeah, buddy," Ally told him. "You try it. You just try it. More than one thing climbing rope's good for. And two can play this game. I seem to remember a man or two I've enjoyed seeing in a harness myself."

Everyone was laughing now. "She's got your number, mate," Koti grinned. "Got one of those fierce ones myself. You're toast."

"I know it," Nate sighed. "Succumbed to the inevitable quite a while ago. No escape once that thunderbolt hits you, try as you might. And I tried. Tried so hard I almost succeeded, and wasn't that a bloody nightmare. Not making that mistake again."

Everyone got quiet for a bit at that, because they all remembered. It hadn't been possible to miss.

"We all stuff up," Liam said, his voice quiet in the dusk that had fallen softly over the garden as they'd sat and talked.

Hannah reached for the matches, but Drew put a restraining hand on hers, got up and walked around lighting citronella candles to keep the mozzies at bay.

The soft glow lit the faces around the tables as Liam continued. "We all make mistakes," he said. "The difference is what happens next."

"When the people you love suffer for your mistakes, though," Nate said, and there was no humor at all in his voice now, "that's the killer, eh."

"You're not the only one who knows about that either," Liam said.

"Not the only one at all." The rasp of Finn's voice now, though the gloom. "Just about every man at this table could tell a tale. Mako's right. Luckily, women have forgiving natures."

"But long memories," Reka said, breaking the somber mood and making everyone laugh. "She'll forgive you, but she'll remind you. That's the price."

"Too true," Hemi sighed. "But ah, well. It's worth it."

marshaling my forces

♡

"Pretty clear that Toro's well and truly taken over that captaincy now," Drew said with a grin down the table at his replacement, seeing the familiar intensity changed to something else now, something looser. Calmer. Nate was beginning to relax a bit in the job, it was clear, at the end of his second season. Finding out that it was possible to have a laugh with his teammates, past and present, and still be the skipper.

Only Drew, of all the men here, fully understood the burden Toro was finally able to lay down. That niggling worry that the selectors had made a mistake, that he wouldn't be up to the job. The dark fear that came at two in the morning, that you couldn't share with anyone.

Although he suspected Toro might be able to share it with Ally. Koti was right, she clearly did have his number. And that support, even if it were unspoken...that mattered. Knowing you had somebody in your corner, win or lose.

It was obvious to Drew, at least, that the selectors hadn't made a mistake. In fact, his opinion had been asked, and he'd given it. Never the biggest player, Toro, but nobody was speedier, or had faster reflexes. He had the quality of every world-class halfback, and had it in spades: the ability to read the game, to change on the fly, to communicate what you saw to the backs, to spur the attack.

A ferocious tackler, too, with heart and courage to burn. Most nines had to be taken off partway through the match, couldn't sustain the pace for the full eighty minutes. Not Toro. He played smart as well as hard, and then there was that x factor. The driving will to win, to excel, to push his performance higher that inspired everyone around him. Which was why he was the skipper.

No matter that the sting was still there when Drew looked at the captain—no longer even the *new* captain—and knew that that was what he was. The captain. The skipper. No matter that Drew might still wish it were him. Wishes weren't horses, and nothing stayed the same. Life rolled on, and a man had to roll with it, and his own life was good. It had been good before, and now it was better.

"You've moved me straight off my course, mate," he told the other man now. "Getting Hannah more help, remember?"

"All right," Reka said promptly. "Tell us what to say, and we'll say it."

"Little kids," Drew reminded her. "New baby. Job. That it's important to keep up with it, and that she needs more help to do it. Not to mention that I need her too. Can't have her being too tired even to talk to me when I come home. Selfish, eh."

"Right," Reka said. "All that. You need more help to do it, Hannah."

"I could've done that," Drew complained. "Come on. Bring something new to the table here. I'm counting on you girls."

"I'll try," Jenna said. "I'm pregnant too, but not as pregnant as Hannah. And I've got a little one too, but not as little as Hannah's. And I'm *not* trying to stay involved professionally right now. So I'm pretty well qualified to talk. I need help. I can't do it by myself. Or I could, but I'd be exhausted. I'm fairly domestic, too—"

"Yeh," Finn said. "Fairly."

She smiled and continued. "But even I know that kids aren't little forever. And whatever Finn thinks, I don't actually want six. Eventually, you run out of babies. And at some point, when the...the hormones settle down, I guess, it's good to have something of your own, but that something's got to be there for you to do. I'm a teacher, and so is Reka. We can go back to that later if we want to, once our kids are older. It's not a hard thing to jump into again. But other careers are harder to do that with. Better to have continuity, I'm sure."

"Money of your own doesn't come amiss either," Kate said bluntly. "Let's be honest. A little power outside the relationship. And let's face it, inside the relationship too."

"Wow. Yep," Ally said. "That's it. I *knew* we needed to come to this party."

"We *are* getting down to it tonight, eh," Nate said. He truly had got comfortable. Talking at Drew's table, and that was good, because there were some divided loyalties here still, and that needed to be put right. This was the perfect opportunity.

"I don't think it's as important for us," Nate went on, "as it is for you girls. That power thing, I mean. We know you have power, job or no, money or no." He got some nods of assent over that. "We're all clear on that one."

"Not easy being the parent when you're doing it alone half the time," Finn said. "Or just being on your own half the time. Pretty sure all of us appreciate that."

"But still," Kate insisted. "Still. I need something that's…mine. Mine to do."

"Which brings us back to the point, doesn't it," Drew said. "Which is that if you're going to do that, do a job of work outside of home, or even *at* home, and you've got kids, you can't do it without help."

"I've got help," Hannah said.

"*More* help. You don't have a mum to live with you, or next to you, or whatever it is that some of them have. Which means you need something else. Nobody's going to think less of you for it, at least nobody who counts. No extra bonus points for scrubbing your own toilets, and who cares if somebody else cooks dinner, long as it gets cooked? I always had somebody to cook my own dinner, do my washing-up *and* my washing, for that matter, before I met you. And scrub my toilets as well. Nobody ever asked me if I was a good enough man because I did. Let alone a good enough dad. Never had to justify it at all. If it helps you work better, and you can afford it, why the hell not? Giving somebody who needs it a job, so you can do your own job. What's wrong with that?"

"Good one, mate," Hemi said quietly.

"Yeh, thanks," he said. "Been thinking about that one."

"Yeah," Kate said, sounding a little belligerent. "Why is that? How come nobody ever asks you guys how you're juggling parenting and rugby? And yet Hannah got asked, you bet she did, in that last totally softball interview. Suddenly, there it is, every time." Her hand hit the table. "Bang. 'How do you manage it all? I'm sure our viewers would love to know.' I never, *ever* saw a post-match interview with you, Drew, where they said, 'So how are you managing to fit in your travel schedule with your family responsibilities, Drew?' Why is that?"

"No idea," he said, a bit taken aback, but that was Kate. "That's what I'm saying. Not fair, and not the way I see it."

"Look what you've stumbled into, Nate," Reka told him. "You may want to take Ally and run right now."

"Nah," he said. "She's already there, no worries. In fact, probably a relief to her."

"It is," she confessed. "I thought I'd have to be some... rugby wife, or something. Whatever that is. I didn't have a clue, other than knowing Kristen. And seeing Hannah some, but Hannah's pretty intimidating."

"I am not," she said.

"You are," Kristen said. "You totally are."

"But I'm..." She struggled with it, and Drew smiled a little, because he knew what they meant, even though he saw the real woman beneath. "I'm nice."

Everyone laughed at that. "And that's worse," Kristen said. "How you've got it all down. That's what Ally's saying. How hard you are to live up to. Just like that show said. How you do all that, and make it look so easy."

"But it's *not* easy," Hannah said. "Of course it's not."

"Which is great to hear," Ally said. "That it's not easy, but you make it work. Because I've got some things I want to do myself too. I'm awfully glad I'm not the only one who thinks that's important."

"Nah. Kate's the other one," Koti said, and everybody laughed.

"Well, WAGs are people too," Reka said staunchly. "And we don't spend our days at the spa, no matter what some people may think."

"So we good?" Drew demanded of Hannah. "Before Kate gets out the placards and organizes the march? We got this sorted? We're going to get somebody set up to come in here every day so you can get back on your feet again, and eventually get back to work, when you're ready? Make it look easy for everybody? Because you just heard them. You've got a reputation to live up to. That's your... your thing. What you're selling."

"That's my brand?" she asked. "Being superwoman?"

"Well, yeah," Kristen said. "One half of the Superpower Couple. Sir Andrew and Lady Callahan."

"If that's your brand," Drew said, "can't tarnish it, can you? Can't have you looking all tired and frazzled during that interview, or having you miss a deadline on one of those launches. We'd better get somebody hired before my mum goes home, I'd say. I'll do the interviewing myself. Whatever it takes."

"Scare them to death," she said.

"Told you. I don't use the Laser Eyes on women. So we good?"

"Single-minded, that's what you are," she sighed. "In front of everybody, too."

"Marshaling my forces," he agreed.

"When you put it like that, it sounds silly," she said. "It's real, the pressure to do it myself. But...maybe you're right."

"We know you've all got dreams too," he said. "You girls support us in ours. Why's it so hard to believe we want to help you do the same? What's wrong with getting you the help you need to do it?"

"All right," she said. "You're *definitely* right. Is that what you want to hear? And yes. Let's do it. Because how can I argue with that?"

He sighed with satisfaction. "I'm right," he informed the table. "I'm *definitely* right. And we're doing it my way. You can all leave now. We're done here."

"Drew!" She laughed. "No."

"When we met Hannah, mate," Hemi informed him, "that first time, Reka and me? We wondered if you could do it. Well, she wondered. I know you better. Now we've all seen how, I reckon. And we're all impressed."

"Wasn't easy," he said.

"So let's hear it," Reka said.

"Let's hear what?" he asked cautiously.

"We heard Finn and Jenna's story today," she said. "And we all know Kate and Koti's, since Koti, as usual, managed to perform for an audience. Some of these fellas even got themselves on tape doing the deed. Including Hemi," she said with a laugh. "At least, I'm pretty sure there were some photos taken. And Liam, and...wait, Koti too. That *was* you carrying Kate down Queen Street," she told Koti. "We weren't surprised at *that*. Not a bit."

"She had a blister," he said, his grin flashing through the gloom. "I parked too far away, and that ring wasn't going to buy itself. No choice."

"Hmm. We've got a bit of a Maori thing going here," Reka said. "You Pakeha boys need to step up your game. Guessing you didn't carry Hannah through the CBD, Drew, or sing her a song in a café either."

"Nah. It was a café, actually. But a bit more private, you're right."

"And?" she prompted.

"What? You want me to tell all of you? Why would you be interested?"

"I'm not," Koti said. "If we're voting."

"Be quiet, Koti," Reka said. "I am. All us girls are. So come on."

"All I'd do is make every other fella here feel good that at least he managed it better than I did," Drew said. "You know I'm rubbish at speeches."

"You are not," Hannah said indignantly. "You make wonderful speeches."

"Well," Hemi conceded, "maybe a bit boring."

"They are not." That was still Hannah, of course.

"All right," Reka said. "You tell us, Hannah."

Hannah looked at him. "All right with you if I do? Because it was *wonderful*."

He sat back and sighed. "Of course. If you want to." He tried to remember what he *had* said. Truth was, he'd been so nervous, he couldn't even remember. He *was* rubbish at speeches, when they mattered. He knew his heart well enough. He just wasn't too good at speaking from it.

"It was a year from the day I met him," she said. "He remembered the day, and the place."

"There you go," Reka said. "That's not rubbish. That's romance. Romance is remembering, because it made an impression. Because *she* made an impression. Romance is remembering, and showing her you do."

"She made an impression." He laughed a little. "She made one hell of an impression. And I didn't say I didn't know what to do. I said I didn't know what to say."

Because, yeh, he'd known what to do. He'd known exactly what to do.

back to the coromandel

♡

It had been ten days since that grueling World Cup victory, since that night when nearly every man here had dug deeper than he ever had, to win a match they should by all rights have lost.

They'd held, and held, and held some more, all their strength long since expended. They'd reached down to the darkest places, found that final reservoir of will, and kept holding. Until the final whistle had blown and they'd been able to stop.

The stadium had erupted. Exploded. And Drew had stood, hands on hips, head down and fighting for breath, and had felt...nothing.

He'd seen Finn embracing Nico, Mako, more players joining the happy mob. The big man sinking to the turf, the tears flowing unchecked and unashamed. The emotion coming so easily to him, always, joy or anger, pain or loss.

Drew had stood alone and felt only relief. That he could stop. That it was over.

It had been the toughest battle of his life. Not just because of the game, but because he'd had the loss of Hannah weighing him down, a dark, cold hole low in his gut. And instead of feeling it, of hurting, had had no choice but to use it to fuel his resolve, his burning need to win. To win this. To win one.

He'd won, in the end. But it had cost him almost everything. And now, he was empty.

Then he'd looked up, had seen her leaning across the barriers to him. Crying. Reaching for him.

A second before, he'd been numb. And then he'd felt so much. So much that, if he'd been a different man, he'd have been on his knees, exactly like Finn. But he wasn't that man. So he'd held her, and laughed, and watched her cry, and had gone off to celebrate with the team. And had come back to her, and known she'd be there.

He'd woken up with her on the first day of their Coromandel holiday, the day he'd scheduled so carefully. The team celebrations over, the Cup shared with an exultant nation on a victory tour from the Bluff to the Cape. And now, released from responsibility, knowing he had eight days with her. Knowing exactly how he wanted to start them. If she said yes.

Of course she'll say yes, his logical, practical side had scolded again on that November morning, the sun already making its presence felt. Hannah was turned away from him in bed, her pale hair streaming across the white pillowcase, a mermaid washed ashore. Her bare foot lying lightly against his calf, because even in sleep, some part of her always seemed to seek him out, to need to touch him, her body and her heart knowing what her mind kept shrinking from. But it was her mind he needed to win. He'd won her heart, he was pretty sure of that, and she'd given her body to him a long time ago. Time to go after that final barrier, bring it crashing down.

She stirred as if she could feel him watching her, rolled over, opened her blue eyes, and smiled, a wide, sleepy, glorious thing. "Morning."

He smiled back, hope surging. "Morning."

♡

He took her kayaking, because that was Step One of his plan. Launched from the golden sand of the beach, pushing her boat off first, then following her. Paddling with easy strokes until they neared the point that marked one end of the curving bay.

A calm sea today, gentle swells taking them for a pleasant, rocking ride. Seabirds flying overhead, a pied shag breaking off, dropping from the sky like an arrow, coming up with a flash of silver in its beak. The sun sparkling on the water, thousands of tiny diamonds against the blue. The sky a paler shade, clear as crystal. A mild breeze caressing his cheek, the water sliding down the paddle onto his hand, cooling his skin.

And the treacherous, deceptive current pulling them inexorably out to sea, just as it had done on that day.

"Stop paddling a moment," he told her.

She lifted her paddle, and he moved his own kayak close to hers with a few draw strokes, then reached for her boat and pulled it next to his. "Grab hold."

"Something wrong?" she asked, doing as he asked, setting her own paddle next to his across the front of their boats, and feeling that current taking them.

"Nah." His throat worked a bit. "Just that this was it. A year ago today. This is the spot where I found you."

"I remember," she said quietly. "I remembered this morning, when you wanted to do this. And when we got in. My first time stepping in the water here since that day. Is that why we're doing it? And was it today? Really?"

"Yeh. It was today. And that's why. Bad idea?"

She looked out past the point, to the Pacific, the vast expanse of blue that stretched all the way to the Americas.

"No," she finally said. "I guess not. Probably good. But hard, remembering. I've been thinking about it. I haven't been able to help it, ever since we got in. I almost asked you to turn around," she confessed. "Because it's hard to remember."

He sat, waited for what she'd say next.

"I was so afraid," she went on at last, "and trying so hard not to be. Trying to believe I'd make it, and knowing somewhere down deep that I wouldn't, but that I was going to keep trying until I couldn't anymore. Wondering how much longer I could struggle, and when I wouldn't have a choice. When I'd have to stop, because I couldn't go on. Trying not to imagine what it would be like to drown. But I knew. I knew it would be…horrible."

"It would have been," he said. "But it didn't happen."

She didn't seem to hear him. "Know what else I thought, afterwards?"

"No, what?"

"I thought, what if it *had* been over? What if that had been my life?"

"And what did you answer?"

She looked out to sea again, the sea that had almost claimed her that day. Had so nearly taken her from him before he'd even had the chance to know her. To love her.

"That I'd spent half my life afraid," she said. "Feeling just like that. I thought I was brave. And I was so wrong."

"You *were* brave," he said. "You *are* brave. You got in the water today. You did that. Didn't even say anything to me. You thought, this is hard, and it's a good thing to do. So you did it. That's courage. And that's you."

She shook her head. "No. I wasn't brave, not then. I hid. I hid behind work, and being right, and being in control, and never taking a chance."

"You came to New Zealand alone," he said. "I'd say that was a chance. And then you took a chance on me."

She turned to him, smiled. "Do you know why I love you?"

He laughed in surprise. "No, but I'd like to. Why?"

"Because you know me so well, and yet you still think that well of me. You think better of me than I do of myself."

"And that's why I love you too," he said. "One of the reasons. Come on. Let's go around the island, ride the waves a bit. Since we're both alive, let's live. Plus," he added practically, "work up an appetite for breakfast."

"So he took you kayaking," Reka said dubiously. "In the spot where you nearly drowned. And that was romantic."

"It was," she protested. "Because it wasn't just the spot where I almost drowned. It was the spot where he saved me."

"Isn't there some group somewhere that believes," Koti said, "that if you save somebody's life, you're responsible for them?"

"Thought you didn't want to hear the story," Drew said.

He shrugged. "Just asking."

"Well," Hannah said, laughing, "that would explain it, maybe. He felt responsible for me that day, anyway. He took me to breakfast. He said that, in fact. That he'd saved me, and now he needed to know I was all right."

"I *said* that," Drew told her. "Of course I said that. What did you expect me to say? 'Glad you didn't drown, and now how about going to bed with me?' How well would that have worked?"

She was actually staring at him, her mouth open. "You did not think that."

"I didn't? Right, then. I didn't. I was being chivalrous. I like your version much better."

"Huh." She still looked surprised, and he had to chuckle a little. "Well, anyway. He took me to breakfast that day, and then he took me to breakfast again, a year later."

"To the same place," Drew said. "Sat in the back garden, at the same table. Had the same breakfast, too."

They'd drunk their coffee while they waited for it, and he'd looked at her across the table from him, her hair in its shining knot, a blue sundress today instead of the yellow one she'd worn that day. And waited.

"What?" she asked, the third time he looked around the lushly planted patio to the little café's entrance. "Are we in a hurry? Or are you starved? We could have eaten back at the house."

"No," he said hastily. "Nothing. So..." He cast about for a topic. "Uh...how's Kristen?"

"How's *Kristen?*" She laughed. "Drew. You don't have to chat. We can just sit."

He grinned at her sheepishly. "Sorry."

"And here's your breakfast," she said as the server approached. "Saved by the bell."

The girl was Italian this time. A romantic, fortunately, because she'd smiled when he'd confided his request, had patted the back of his hand and promised him, "Yes. It will be done."

"Not the one with the tomatoes," he'd thought to add. "The one with just the eggs."

"*Sì,*" she'd said. "I understand."

Now, the girl set the plate in front of Hannah, turned to Drew and deposited his own, gave him a wink and a smile, and walked off. Drew had a suspicion she might be watching from the doorway, but that was all right. There was nobody else back here this early, he'd seen with relief. One Italian girl—that was all right. One girl, and Hannah.

She didn't eat, though, just took another sip of coffee, finally picked up her toast and took a nibble. And... nothing.

Maybe they'd stolen it, Drew thought wildly, wanting to look around to see, but needing to watch Hannah. The waitress and the cook were probably on their way to Auckland right now. Splitting the profits. Aw, shit. He'd never even considered that. He'd been living in New Zealand too long.

"Aren't you hungry after all?" she asked in surprise.

"What?"

She gestured with her fork at his still-laden plate. "Your breakfast."

"Oh." He picked up his own fork, dug in. "Nah. Starved. You should eat too."

She laughed. "I am eating."

"More. You should eat more."

Time stretched out as he plowed determinedly through his own breakfast, watched her make agonizingly slow inroads into her own. He held his breath when she finally picked up the second triangle of toast, and...still nothing.

Definitely on their way to Auckland.

She took another bite of egg, and then a comical expression twisted her lips, her blue eyes going wide.

"What?" he asked.

She held the serviette to her mouth, spat something into it. "I think I chipped a tooth. There's a *bone* or something in here. In my eggs!" She reached a cautious finger into her mouth, felt around.

"All right?" he asked.

"Yes," she said with relief. "I think so. Nothing jagged or anything. What *was* that?" She folded the serviette back to check. Then sat, breath held, and stared.

They hadn't taken it to Auckland. They'd put it under the eggs. And it was sitting in her serviette now. His ring. Her ring. He hoped.

"Drew." Her eyes had flown back to his. "It's..."

"Yeh," he said, tried to laugh. "They were meant to put it under the toast. Sorry."

She was scrubbing at it now. "Oh, Drew. And I almost *swallowed* it."

He had to smile. "Glad you didn't. That wouldn't have been too romantic, getting it back."

"No," she said, succumbing to a fit of the giggles. "We'd have had to..."

"Yeh," he said. "A bucket, I reckon."

"Oh," she gasped, laughing harder. "Oh. *Disgusting.*" Which made him laugh too, and so much for his romantic moment.

"Well," she said, wiping her eyes with the clean serviette he handed her. "That was...novel."

"Now that you have it," he said, his heart galloping in his chest again, "how about if I put it on you?"

She still had it in her hand, and now she looked at it for the first time. "Is it..."

"Yeh." His mouth was dry despite the water he'd just drunk, because there wasn't enough water in the world for this. "It is. It's me asking you to marry me. It's me asking if I can put that ring on your finger, and keep it there."

"Are you sure?"

He had to laugh again. Only Hannah would answer a proposal that way. "I'm sure, sweetheart. I've been sure for a good long while now. The question is, are you."

He waited, his heart in his throat. Wanted to say something else, and didn't know what. Because it wasn't up to him. It was up to her.

Finally, she spoke. "I said I'd spent half my life scared. I'm not spending the rest of it like that."

That was good, and he was glad, but it didn't answer the question.

"From now on," she said, "I'm taking the risk. I've gone through my life saying no. Not yet. Not me. Not now. That's not going to be me anymore. If it's worth it, if I want it, I'm saying yes."

She was handing the ring back across the table to him, and his own hand went out for it. She wasn't going to take it. She was saying yes, but she was telling him no?

He stared at her, took his ring back, and waited.

"Please," she said. "Please put it on me, Drew. Because I'm saying yes."

♡

"And that's what he did," Hannah told Reka proudly, turning the huge diamond on her finger.

Reka had her hands at her chest. "Aw. That's so sweet. Who knew?"

"Course, she said the diamond was too big," Drew said with a crooked grin. "Wanted me to switch it out."

"Better than telling you it was too small," Reka said. "Easy premarital test. If she says it's too small, you need a prenup. What did you say to that?"

He laughed. "I said no."

In fact, he'd got her in his lap and kissed her good and properly, for once heedless of watching eyes, until she was melting, sighing and whimpering into his mouth. Then he'd taken her home, put her on his bed, taken everything off her but the ring, and done his utmost to convince her that he was her man, and he always would be.

Long and slow, kisses and touches and soft murmurs in the warmth of late morning. Until he was threading his fingers through hers, sliding into her, hearing her gasp and seeing her eyes stretch wide. Just like that first time. Just like the best times.

He'd felt the ring on her finger against his own skin, had looked into those blue eyes, and had known that it was true, and it was real. And had known, finally, that she knew it too.

poetic justice

♡

An hour later, and Nate was pulling out of Drew and Hannah's drive and turning left, back toward Mt. Maunganui and the hotel.

Hemi and Reka, Koti and Kate had stayed behind to clean up, but otherwise, there'd been a general exodus. Not too late at all, because of all the pregnant partners. A whole new world.

Just as well, because as a crash course in WAGdom, the day had been pretty intense, he suspected. He and Ally had done a bit of socializing with his Hurricanes teammates, of course, but this was a different level.

He looked across at Ally. She'd been quieter than usual tonight. A bit subdued, but then, that was to be expected, even from somebody as outgoing as Ally.

"All right?" he asked her. "Not too bad?"

"A little overwhelming," she admitted, conforming his suspicions. "Easier than I thought it would be, though. I always figured Drew and Hannah were just nice to me because of Kristen. But they're all that way."

"You know me," he pointed out. "You know Mako."

"Yeah, and how different are the two of you? You can see why I wasn't sure. Especially about Finn. He's pretty frightening."

"Finn?" Nate laughed. "Not exactly. He's like Mako. A hard man on the paddock, and a pussycat off it. Just like me."

She scoffed. "Oh, yeah. You're some pussycat."

"Working on it. Very nearly human by now." He cast a cautious look behind him, merged onto the motorway.

"Let's not go back," she said. Impulsively, of course, because that was how she said everything. "Let's go for a drive. And a swim."

"Don't have our togs," he said. "Or any towels, even."

"So?"

He glanced at her again, saw that look in her eye, and he had a feeling he was going to be doing something he'd regret, and not regret at all, before this night was over.

"What, is my big, tough rugby captain too chicken to skinny-dip with me?" she teased with her best saucy smile. "Afraid you'll get cold? Afraid you won't be able to think of any way to warm up? Or are you afraid you won't be able to warm *me* up?"

He laughed again, happiness bubbling up like champagne. "One week engaged to you. One *week*. And you're already getting me into trouble."

"You never know," she said. "Maybe you'll get *me* into trouble, if I'm very, very lucky. Seems to me I got you a little carried away once or twice."

"I am controlled," he pointed out. "I am disciplined."

"Oh, yeah," she said. "You just tell yourself that. Right up until you're not."

She got him. She always got him. "So, drive?" he said. "Beach?"

She snuggled down into her seat with a little sigh of satisfaction. "I knew I could talk you into it."

He smiled again, swung off the motorway, went through a roundabout and was on it again, headed east this time. He punched the button for the moon roof and let the night fill the car.

Darkness outside, and Ally in the car with him, wanting an adventure. And in what universe wasn't that a wonderful thing?

"Maketu Beach," he decided. "Much more private. Take us about twenty minutes. Why don't you find us some music? Get us in the mood."

"To swim?" she asked.

"Yeh." He smiled at her. "Music to…swim by."

Ten minutes in, and the music, the night were working for him. His headlights splitting the darkness, and they hadn't met another car for kilometers. And the thought of what was to come. The inky blackness of the nighttime sea, the cool of the water. And Ally.

Who wasn't able to wait, clearly. Something about the night, the music, the mood had got her going too, because her right hand was on his knee. And it was moving.

He glanced across at her, turned his eyes hastily back to the road as he felt himself drifting. He corrected, then found himself taking his foot off the gas entirely.

She'd switched hands. The one wearing his ring was on the inside of his thigh now, and she had the other one on the back of his neck. The hair was standing up there, and everything else was stirring too. Her touch did something to him. Every single time.

"I love watching you drive," she said, caressing him with her hands, her voice. "I loved watching you tonight, too. Did I say that? How proud I am of you? How much I like being with you?"

"Ally," he said, as sternly as he could manage. "Slow down."

It was his Captain's Voice, and it didn't work a bit. She laughed, and now her hand was up higher, and he swerved again, swore, slowed a little more. Her hand moved, stroked, and his foot hit the gas just like the rest of his body did.

There had been headlights behind him for a while now. He eased off the gas again, fighting for that self-control.

He'd let the fella pass, he decided. Five more minutes, and they'd be at the beach. If they even made it out of the car. But he didn't think he was the best choice for leading the way there.

The car didn't pass, though. Instead, it turned on its own lights. The flashing blue ones.

"Aw, sh—", Nate breathed. Why tonight?

Ally looked around. "Maybe he's going somewhere," she said hopefully. "An ambulance."

A blip from the siren put paid to that idea. Nate sighed and pulled onto the shoulder, stopped the car, and sat.

He looked across at Ally. "Don't even say it."

"What?" she asked innocently, then spoiled the effect by giggling. "You mean you might actually get a ticket? *You?* I didn't think that was allowed. I thought you were disciplined."

"I used to be." He pushed the button for the window as the officer approached.

He man bent down to peer into the window. "Evening," Nate said.

"Evening," he got in return. "May I see your documents, please?"

Nate handed them over, and the man pulled out a flashlight, scrutinized them.

Nate waited. "Quit smiling," he hissed at Ally.

"Sorry," she said, made a poor attempt at schooling her expression, and failed.

"Nate Torrance," the officer said.

Nate sighed. "Yeh. That's me."

"Not doing so well, are you?" the man asked. "How many have you had tonight?"

"Two beers," Nate said. He knew that everyone said "two beers." It was just that in his case, it happened to be the truth.

"I'll have to ask you step out of the car," the man said.

Nate sighed again, got out, went back to the police car and endured the breathalyzer test. His first one ever, and bloody hell, but it was embarrassing.

"Huh." The officer read the results. "Barely a reading. It really was two beers, eh."

"Yeh," Nate said. "It was. I don't drive drunk."

"Wouldn't have thought so. But the way you were driving...Want to explain that?"

Nate scratched the back of his neck. The neck that Ally had had her soft fingers on just minutes before.

"I got...engaged last week," he said reluctantly.

"Ah," the man said. "That the young lady?"

"Well, yeh." Nate glared. "Of course it is."

"Sorry," the man said hastily. "You never know."

"And she's..." Nate stopped. How was he meant to explain this?

"Yeh," the man said. "She is." He saw Nate glaring and coughed. "I mean, pretty girl. Congratulations."

"Look," Nate said. "I know I wasn't driving too well. Let's just say I'm going to get where we're going in about five minutes, and I won't be slowing down any more along the way. I've got someplace I need to be."

The man was frankly grinning now. "Ah. Been married nearly fifteen years myself. Early days, eh."

"Yeh," Nate said with a sheepish grin. "And just back from the Tour. It's all a bit...exciting."

The officer nodded, walked him back to the car. Nate got in without a word to Ally, shoved the documents into the glove box, and waited.

"Are you going to give him a ticket?" Ally asked.

"Nah," the man said. "Not tonight. Call it a warning."

"Really." She actually looked disappointed, Nate thought with outrage. "Because you're right," she said hopefully. "He wasn't driving very well."

The officer looked at Nate, and he read sympathetic amusement in the other man's eyes. "Could be he had a little provocation," he said. "You take care he does better, miss."

She sighed. "How come you guys never say that to me?"

The professional mask had slipped entirely, and he was laughing. "I'll say congrats and send you on your way," he told Nate. "Get her there safely, mate, and don't take too long about it. And best of luck."

♡

"Well, I call that disappointing," she pronounced when he'd pulled onto the road again, was driving his usual cautious kilometer or two below the limit.

"Do not push me," he warned her. "Most embarrassing moment of my life."

"Really?" she asked with pleasure. "The very most? Man, you really have lived way too safely."

He laughed. He couldn't help it. "You're going to be the death of me. Or the making of me, I can't tell which."

She smiled happily back. "I'll do my best—my very best—to be both. How soon until we go swimming?"

"Two minutes." He could see the sign for Maketu in the distance. "Two minutes, and then I take you for your swim, and you find out what happens to naughty girls who get naked on the beach."

on the mount

♡

She could have been more tactful, Kate thought a bit guiltily as she and Koti said their goodbyes and climbed into the back seat of Reka and Hemi's car for the short drive home. But she'd *meant* to be tactful.

She sighed. No way around it, tact wasn't her strong suit. She'd just have to apologize to Koti when they were alone.

And all right, apologizing wasn't her strong suit either. But she'd do it anyway. Because, yeah. Tact.

"Good time," Hemi said from the driver's seat. "Good to have all the boys together again, and good to see Nate settling in so well too. Good to show everybody that the guard's well and truly changed, and that everybody's all right with that."

"Harder for us than for you, I sometimes think," Reka said. "Hannah's right. It's better for us to have our own lives, our own focus. Important to remember that we're about more than what you do and who you are. And, yeh, about Nate. Settling in, I thought, and settling down as well."

"No hope for it," Hemi agreed, then laughed at her snort. "Nah. He's a happier man all around. That's easy to see."

He turned into the quiet street dominated by the massive Moreton Bay fig that took up a lot-sized space at the corner, then was taking the turn into the semi-circular driveway, pulling up in front of the sprawling modern home he shared with Reka and their four children, with her mum cozily ensconced in her own granny flat.

"D'you mind popping in and checking on Maia for us?" Koti asked as they all got out of the car.

"Why?" Reka asked. "You not coming in?"

"Thought I'd take Kate for a drive," Koti said.

There was something in his voice that told Kate her apology was definitely going to be required, and that she'd been wrong. She was going to enjoy it.

"Oh, yeah?" she asked. "Going to show me the stars?"

"Something like that."

"We won't wait up, eh," Reka said.

"Probably best," he agreed cordially. "See you in the morning."

♡

"Hmm." Hemi used his key on the front door as Koti's flash car swung through the drive and out onto the street. He stood aside and held the door for Reka. "I think Kate's about to get reacquainted with Koti's um."

"Got your mind right in that gutter, boy," Reka said. "Maybe he really does want to look at the stars."

"Yeh, right." He shut the door behind them and grabbed her from behind. He felt her start of surprise as he pulled her back against him, then the softening in her body when he bent to nuzzle the side of her neck, because she loved that, and he loved doing it to her. "Got something disparaging you'd like to say about my um?" he murmured in her ear. "Because I'd truly love to have an excuse to put you right tonight."

He heard the *thud* as she dropped her purse to the tiled floor of the entryway, the hitch in her breath as his mouth continued to move over her skin, as his hand came around to find a full breast. This just never got old.

"Why don't we just...pretend I did something wrong?" she got out. "Then you can show me what a warrior you are. Because I miss those Northern Tours."

"What?" His hand stopped moving, and he lifted his head. "You miss me being gone for five weeks?"

"Not that," she said, snuggling up to him a little more. "Touch me again. Don't stop. Please."

"Not until you explain that," he said sternly. He wanted to. Oh, yeh. He wanted to. But she wanted to have some fun too? He'd oblige.

"All right, then," she sighed. "If I have to. I miss you coming home. Having all that pent-up ferocity for me. I miss you showing me everything you wanted, everything you'd thought of. Sending the kids to Mum's and keeping me in bed for days. I ended up pregnant half the time. And I loved it."

"Mmm." His hand was there again now, and she was leaning back against him, purring her contentment. "Right, then. I can't take myself off for five weeks. But I've got some things I've thought of, no worries. So let's go. Upstairs. I hope you're ready to learn, because I'm ready to take you to school."

♡

"All right," Kate said when they'd turned at the fig tree, were on the main road again. "You didn't have to go to this extreme. I was planning to apologize anyway."

She looked across at him, saw the flash of a smile, and relaxed a little. He hadn't said anything since they'd got in the car, and for a minute there, she'd wondered.

"Oh, for the apology I've got in mind," he told her, his voice silky smooth, "we needed the car."

"All right, now I'm completely at a loss. Why? So you can yell?"

"Nah. So you can."

That shut her up. And instantly flipped the switch, had blood rushing everywhere it needed to be.

He drove for ten minutes or so, the silence becoming more fraught with every kilometer.

"Where are we going?" she finally asked.

"The Mount."

"All...right. Why?"

"You ask a lot of questions, don't you? Never mind. You'll find out."

She couldn't handle the silence. She knew he was playing, but there was an edge, too, she could tell. She wasn't sure if it made her nervous or excited. All right, she was sure. It made her both.

"Everybody knows I was just being funny," she told him. "And anyway, what about that reputation of yours? You got that the old-fashioned way. You earned it. So if anybody thinks anything at all about you, it's because of you, not me. And all right, I didn't say it quite right, but that's because it didn't come out quite the way I meant it. It sounded much better in my head."

He was winding up the streets of the extinct volcano that gave Mt. Maunganui its name, then pulling to a stop off the road near the summit. With, indeed, a view out to the dark sea below, the lights of the town and Papamoa beyond glittering to the southeast, Tauranga to the southwest, and the distant dots that were the smaller settlements to the northwest. The entire hilltop reserve deserted now, past ten on a Sunday night.

"This is the place, huh," she said.

"Yeh," he said. "This is the place. So you can stop chattering. You realize you are, don't you?"

"Well, if you'd talk to me, I wouldn't have to. Why here?"

"It's a good spot," he said with a shrug. "See some lights, some stars too. Quiet."

"Uh-huh. And you know this how?"

She got a low chuckle out of him for that. "Never you mind."

"Mm-hmm. Thought so. Because the All Blacks do some training here. And because, once upon a time, you used to bring girls up here. Now let's get this clear again? I'm in big trouble because I joked about you not being enough of a super stud, to your teammates who were all *with* you when those things happened? What is wrong with this picture?"

"You think that's what this is?" he asked, and he actually sounded surprised.

"Well, of course I think that's what it is. What else have I been…chattering about, all the way up here?"

"Well, I wondered," he admitted. "Nah. It's not what they know. It's what you know."

"Oh." She laughed. "Me? Oh, I'm convinced, big boy. You're all good with me."

"I will be. Soon as you get out of the car and climb into the back seat." He sighed. "I did you bent over the kitchen sink the night I got home from the Tour. I thought that'd hold you, but apparently not. So get back there."

She opened her mouth for another smart retort, shut it again. Who was she kidding? "You're going to make me apologize really hard, aren't you?" she asked, making her voice small.

"Baby," he promised, "you're going to be apologizing so hard it hurts."

She shivered.

"Now," he said softly, "third time I've asked. Go get in that back seat and wait for me."

"Fine," she sighed, putting on a little show even as the excitement began to build.

He didn't move, just sat and watched her in the dark as she opened her door, got out, slammed it again with a little too much force, then climbed into the back and shut that door. Hard.

"Happy?" she asked. "Enjoying that?"

"Oh, yeh," he said. "But not as much as I will be."

"Just going to keep talking," she asked, "or were you thinking about delivering?"

"You are just asking for it, aren't you?" he asked.

"Only if you've got it."

He still didn't move fast. He took the keys from the ignition, set them in the center console, reached back for his wallet and added that to the mix. At last, he opened his door and got out, opened the back door and unfastened Maia's car seat, set it in the front, and, finally, was getting into the back seat and shutting the door. Gently.

"Not exactly the world's sexiest moment," she said. "The car seat and all."

She was doing her best to be snarky even as her entire body was humming, the heat pooling. He didn't say anything, just looked across at her, unsmiling. Then he turned to face her, and she quivered.

She expected him to touch her. Well, to be truthful, she expected him to grab her. Instead, he ran a hand over her hair, down her jawline, his thumb tracing the curve of her lips, and they parted as if they'd been waiting for him. Treacherous, thinking they answered to him. His thumb slipped inside, an alien presence, and she gasped a little, bit down gently, sucked on it. Her mouth again, betraying her.

"Aw, that's good," he said. "You know what you're going to be doing tonight, don't you?"

Another surge of heat, and his hand had slid on down, his fingertips brushing her throat, then going around to cup the back of her neck, stroke the sensitive spot at the edge of her hairline. Gripping her there, not hard, just enough to let her know he was holding her, that he had her.

"Take your shirt off," he told her. Still quiet, but so sure.

"You not undressing me?" she asked. "Thought this was all about control."

"Oh, I think if I tell you to do it, watch you do it, that's exactly what it is, don't you? Go on. Take it off for me. Not too fast."

He sat back and watched. She tossed her hair back, got two hands under the snug red top—red, because he loved it—and pulled it up her body.

She had her arms crossed in front of her, the shirt over her face, when she felt his hand again. On her side, at the curve of her waist. She gasped, stopped, because his thumb was stroking again, his hand moving up, cupping her breast.

"Not that I don't like you like that," he said, and she heard the amusement in his voice, "but I told you to take it off."

She pulled it over her head, dropped it to the floor. She was wearing only her bra, a short skirt, and heels. As usual.

"Nice," he said. "But that gave me another idea. For your apology." He flicked the clasp of her bra with a practiced hand, pulled it off, but didn't drop it to the floor with her shirt. Instead, he took a wrist in each hand, then, to her shock, pulled them behind her back, wrapped the skimpy bra around them, and she felt the knot going in. Tight.

"Ah," he said, "that's better. That's brilliant."

"Koti." She was wriggling, tugging. He'd tied her too well, though, and she couldn't get her hands free.

"All right," she said, looking up and shaking her hair back from her face. "You've made your point."

"Baby," he said, "I haven't even started making my point." He had both hands around her waist, was shifting her against the door.

He was over her, his hands on her breasts, and her bound hands were grabbing behind her for the armrest, holding on, because his mouth was at her throat, kissing, biting, exactly the way she loved, the way that drove her crazy. And then that talented mouth was moving lower, kissing and biting its way, settling on her, and she couldn't help it, she was arching towards him. He knew exactly how to fondle her, how to tease her, and she was squirming for real now.

"Somebody's going to...come," she managed to say.

"Somebody's going to come, all right," he told her. "And it's going to be you. Over and over again. Until you can't take it anymore, and you're begging me to stop."

"Koti..." she moaned.

He had a hand on her foot, was wrenching off one heel, then the other, then pulling her skirt off. Not quite as much finesse now, not quite as far in control as he was pretending to be.

"Nervous about showing yourself?" he asked her when she was lying against the door wearing only the tiny cocoa-colored bikini panties.

"Yes," she managed, barely knowing what she was saying.

"Then we'll leave these on, shall we?"

"No," she said. "Take them off and…please. Please."

"Too easy," he said. "Too fast. And we're staying here a while. I need a good, long, hard apology. And you're going to be tied up for every bit of it. But that's not going to work so well for me. I don't think I can wait that long. So I'm afraid we're going to have to put that pretty mouth to work. Give me some relief, so I can work you over hard enough."

He was reaching across her, working the levers of the passenger seat, moving it all the way forward, tilting the seatback as well.

"Give you some room to move," he said. "That's important."

He reached for her, lifted her, lowered her so she was on her knees on the floor of the car, then slid around her, sat back against the seat, and unzipped.

Her heart was beating hard, and she could hear her panting breath in her ears. Was she willing to do this? With her wrists tied behind her back, in a car?

He wasn't giving her a choice, though. One part of her mind told her she had one, that she could ask him to stop any time, and he'd stop. And the other part shut that reasonable voice down, because she didn't want to hear it. She wanted to play Koti's game. All his games. So she let him take her head in his hands, guide her to him. She let him hold her there, let him tell her what to do, listened to the groaned commands, and obeyed them. Every one of them.

"Aw, baby," he gasped at last. "Aw, come on. Take it all. Come on. Do it."

And she did. She felt the shuddering in his body, nearly choked at the force of it, but didn't. She took all of him, swallowed, and swallowed again. And loved it.

♡

He lay back and breathed hard, looked down at her. Sitting back, her arms twisted behind her back, looking up at him. Licking her lips, her tongue coming out to wash her chin. And a smile on her face.

He'd tied her up and made her do it. He couldn't believe it. And he couldn't believe he wasn't sorry.

He reached into the console, grabbed a water bottle, held it for her, watched her take a long drink, her throat moving, washing him down, and loved watching it.

"Done?" he asked, careful not to choke her.

She nodded, and he took it back and took a drink himself.

"Not going to untie me?" she asked.

"Not a chance. Unless it's hurting," he thought to say. "Is it hurting?"

"No."

"Then you're staying tied for me. Because damn, baby, but that's exciting. Bet you're wet, aren't you? Because you loved that."

"Yes." It was a sigh.

She was loving being tied up, too, he could tell. He shifted around her, got his hands around her waist, pulled her up onto the seat, and propped her against the door again like a doll. His doll.

"Know I said you could keep the undies," he told her. "But I lied." He touched her there, two fingers rubbing over her center, saw her back arch, her body strain.

"So wet," he told her. "I'm taking them off."

He did. And then he ran his hands up her thighs, spread her legs for him, and that was even better.

"Now I'm afraid you really are naked," he told her. "All exposed like this. Good thing, because I need to spend some time here. And I get to do it, don't I?"

"Yes," she said breathlessly. "Yes. Please."

He'd muffled her pretty comprehensively before, but there was no quieting her now. He had his hands, his mouth on her, and she was twisting under him, her back arching, her hips trying to lift into him, her broken cries echoing through the car. He moved faster, got her closer, slowed down just to make her squirm some more. Got his fingers inside her, found the spot that made her wild, pressed on it as his tongue teased the exact place, the best place, until she was straining at the limit of her bonds, keening.

And then he stopped.

"Koti," she begged. "Koti. I need to…I need to come. I need it so bad."

"No," he said. "You need to come hard. And I'm going to make you come so hard. Start you up again, stop you just before you get there. Over and over and over again, until I say you can come. I told you you were going to pay. This is where you do it."

He did what he promised. By the time he allowed her to climb that final time, she was shaking, moaning, and his face and hands were slick with her.

"Pleeeeease." It was one long moan, all she could say.

"You going to be good?" he asked her. "Do what I say?"

"Yes. Yes." She was trembling, shaking. "Please let me. Please."

He smiled. Started again, and this time, when she climbed, so impossibly high, out there on the edge, at the very peak, he let her go. He let her fly.

♡

She thought it would never stop. The spasms racked her, again and again, for what seemed like minutes on end. It had never, surely never been like this. And then he was on her again, urging her up, and she was going again. Over and over and over, just as he'd promised. Until she was shaking, until she was nearly crying, trying to pull her hands free, the bondage merely increasing the almost unbearable sensation.

"Stop," she finally gasped. "Stop."

He stopped, exactly as she'd known he would, as soon as she asked. He sat up, pulled her against his chest, held her until the trembles died down, until she wasn't shaking anymore.

She felt his hands working behind her back and realized he was releasing her, and then he was pulling her arms around in front of her, massaging them.

"Sorry," he said. "I forgot, tell you the truth. I mean, I remembered at the beginning." He laughed a little. "I enjoyed it, too. And then...I forgot. Would've untied you, though, if you'd said. You all right?"

"Yes," she said. In truth, she was a bit uncomfortable. She wriggled her arms, let him work them until the sensation eased.

"I'm naked in a car," she said with wonder. "Stark naked in a car, in the middle of the city. And you've still got all your clothes on. How do I let you talk me into these things?"

♡

He knew how. He knew exactly how, and he was about to do it some more. He pulled her into his lap, kissed her, then kept doing it, heard the little noises she made into his mouth, the muffled sounds of desire, and his own need twisted up that little bit higher.

Her smart mouth, and her obedient little body. What a delicious combination.

It was the first time he'd kissed her all night, he realized. He hadn't been too focused on the romance, that was for sure. He had the feeling, as much apologizing as he was making her do tonight, that he was going to have to do some making up of his own later. But that was all right. That would be good too.

"That my prize?" she murmured when he pulled back, her mouth so soft, a little swollen, and that was so good. "I get a kiss for doing so well?"

"Yeh," he told her, smoothing her hair again. "You were a very good girl. But I was thinking something else. Because you're still naked."

"Mm. Because you took all my clothes off."

"I did. And I'm afraid you're going to have to keep them off a while longer. And that I'm going to need this again." He picked up the bra, grabbed her wrists in one hand, in front of her body this time, wrapped the stretchy band around them.

"Koti," she protested, wriggling in his lap, trying to pull her hands out of his grasp, and if anything had ever been hotter than this, he didn't know what it would be.

"Shh," he said, tying the thing more securely. "Last part of your apology. Because I loved this. And you loved it too. Now let's see just how sorry I can make you."

He grabbed her hips, held her down. "Quit squirming, baby. You're going to get all the squirming you can take in a minute here. I promise."

She was breathing hard again, and damn, but he was turned on. He lifted her easily, turned her to face him.

"Straddle me," he told her, and she did it.

He had her hips in his hands again, was guiding her onto him, pushing her down, impaling her on him, and bloody hell, but it felt good. So warm, so tight around him.

She let out a long moan as he did it that went straight through him, and that made it even better. Her bound hands forced her to lean forward, lift her arms high, behind his head, rest her elbows against the back of the seat, which put her beautiful little breasts at exactly the right level. He was holding her in place with his hands, his mouth, moving her over him as if all that mattered was what he needed from her. And feeling what that did to her.

Harder now, faster, and she was keening again, letting herself be used for his pleasure, and wanting it that way.

He needed her to come. He needed it now. He was climbing, and it was so much better when she was there too. He got a hand in there, shoved her away from him with the other hand, held her tight, and rubbed.

"Tell me you're sorry," he ordered her.

"I'm...sorry," she gasped.

"Tell me, 'yes, Koti.' Tell me to do it. Tell me."

"Oh...Yes, Koti. I'm sorry. I'm..." She could barely say it. "S-s-sorry. I'm...Please. Do it. Please do it harder."

The need was hauling at him, grabbing him in an iron fist, squeezing him, pulling him up, and up higher. "Show me. Now."

"Sorrryyyyyy."

It was a wail, and she was all the way there, bucking, and he grabbed her hips again, shoved her over him, again and again. Took every last centimeter of her. Took it all the way.

♡

He helped her get dressed again, afterwards. Kissed her, joked, was his usual sweet self. But she was shaken to the core.

He saw it, after a minute. She had a hand on the door handle, wanting to get out, to get into the front, but he scooted over next to her and put a restraining hand on her arm.

"Kate. Wait."

She turned, and he opened his arms, pulled her into him, and held her.

"What's wrong?" he asked gently. "Too rough? Too much after all? You can always say no, baby. You can always say no."

"That's not it." She pulled away from him again, even though being in his arms felt so good. She needed to see his face for this, and for him to see hers. "It's that I didn't want to say no."

"And what's wrong with that?" he demanded. "'Yes' sounded pretty bloody good to me."

"I don't know if that's…" She swallowed. "What that means. I'm not that kind of person."

"What kind of person?"

She looked straight at him. "A submissive person."

He didn't sigh, didn't look exasperated, to her relief. She couldn't have handled his dismissing this.

"No," he said. "You're not. Except maybe in bed. There, I'd say, yeh, you are. And like I said—works for me. And that's all that matters. Works for you, works for me. Anything we do together, anything we both want to do, is all right. Sometimes it'll be sweet. Sometimes it'll be wild. And sometimes, like tonight, it'll be right up to our edge. Because we want to. Nobody gets to say but us. Nobody gets to judge but us."

"You like it the other way, too, right?" she asked. "Sweet?"

"I like it every way we do it," he promised. "Every single way. There's never once been a time we've made love and I've thought, nah, didn't like that one."

She laughed, the tension loosening its grip. "Yeah. Me neither."

"You're worried about something else too, though," he said slowly. "You're worried that I really am saying you're powerless here. That because I tied you, and you liked it, and I did too, that something's changed. But it hasn't."

"You mean I still get to boss you around sometimes, make you complain?"

"You still get to boss me around. I promise. Long as I get you to boss you around too. Later. Even the score a bit."

"Oh, new perspective," she said. "I like that."

"Mm. Thought you would. And besides," he went on, so casually that her antennae went straight up, "I thought we wanted another baby. And I was reading up on it. They say the female orgasm may help pull the sperm into the uterus. Just doing my bit to send my boys along their way so they can get the job done."

She stared at him in disbelief. "You did not read that."

"Yeh," he said, and there was no doubt about it what-soever, he was grinning, looking smug. Looking pleased as punch. "I did. Figured, best effort, and all that. Because somebody taught me that. That if I really want something, I need to go after it. Not stop until I get it."

She sighed, tried to pretend to be annoyed. "So I'm just a baby-makin' machine, huh? That the deal? That what that was?"

He laughed, gave her a soft kiss, cuddled her close.

"No," he said when her cheek was pressed to his heart. "You're the woman who keeps me up to the mark, the one who keeps me on my toes. You're my gut check and my conscience and my heart. You're the lover I wanted more than I've ever wanted a woman, the one who still sets me on fire."

He pulled back, tugged her shirt a little straighter, smoothed her hair where their exertions had rumpled it. "And one more thing," he told her with that smile that still worked so well on her, every single time. "You make a pretty fair baby. And I want you to make mine."

a holiday project

♡

Reka was lying on the still-made bed with Hemi. On top of the duvet, because they hadn't even managed to pull it back.

"That was nice," she sighed. She propped herself on an elbow, traced the whorls of his tattoo on his heavy chest with a finger, following the intricate blue-black pattern laid over his bronzed skin all the way around to the bulk of his shoulder, down his arm. She'd traced it a million times. She could have drawn it by now. And she still loved touching it. His moko. Her man.

She drew a chuckle out of him. His own hand was still moving lazily down her own shoulder blade, all the way to her waist, holding her there. "Nice? I give it that much grunt, and I get 'nice?'"

"All right," she said, smiling down at him. "It was awesome. How's that?"

"Better. I'll keep thinking those five-weeks-without-you thoughts, that the idea? Or maybe the opposite." He had that look in his eyes now. "Better yet, we could change it up, challenge ourselves. Always a good way to up your game. Seeing Hugh and Josie, Nate and Ally just starting out—maybe we need to remember how that was. Maybe we should see if we can do it every night for a month. Course, we'd have to get creative, keep from boring ourselves to tears. No more quick-and-easy, get off and go to sleep, just because we know what buttons to push."

"I like that," she said, the thought stirring her, because that's what Hemi still did to her. "A challenge. One night could be your night, next mine. Our choice."

"Ah." That was definitely a light in his brown eyes now. "So it's ask-you-anything time, is it?"

"Choose your own adventure," she suggested. "You're on holiday. Why not?"

"And if a kid gets sick, something like that," he said, "that gets tacked onto the end."

She sighed. "Coaching again. Rules."

"Setting expectations." His hand was on her thigh now, letting her know he still liked touching it, even after four babies. "And we don't even have to worry about birth control," he pointed out. "Total spontaneity, soon as we lock that bedroom door." Another sigh, this one a heartfelt one. "I love being married."

"Not what you said after the vasectomy."

That got a groan out of him. "Because I thought I'd never want to do it again. You just took all the magic out of the moment. Cheers for that."

She laughed. "Got until tomorrow to get the magic back. Tomorrow your night, or mine?"

"Oh, ladies first," he said, and she was right, the magic was going to be back. Right back.

"To clarify," she said, "because I know how you coaches like to have everything clear. 'My turn' just means I get to ask for what I want, eh. Even if it's something you do."

"Let's hope so," he said. "Because my turn is *definitely* going to include some things you do. Even if that's just 'bend over.'"

She shivered, and he saw it and smiled. "Because I love that," he said, giving her bum a healthy slap. "Definitely going to be choosing that a time or two. I do enjoy a holiday project."

She hummed a bit more, and they got ready for sleep together, crawled under that duvet at last, the nighttime house silent around them.

"That was sweet tonight," she said when they were lying in the dark, his heavy arm across her chest, holding her safe. Her favorite way to fall asleep. "Hearing about Hannah and Drew. Wasn't it?"

"Mmm," he agreed.

"He doesn't talk much," she said. "Never has. But he does all the right things."

"That's what counts." He sounded pretty sleepy now.

"Still glad you talk more," she told him. "But, yeh. You're right. Talking's good, but what you do counts more. Knowing that you're there for me." She tugged his arm more tightly around herself. "Seeing Drew tonight, how sweet he was, with her so close to the baby…it made me think about when Ariana was born."

"What did I say then? Can't remember. Remember crying a bit, that's all. Don't think I did much else, other than be terrified and try not to show it."

"Yeh." She smiled, there in the dark, snuggled a little closer. "You did cry. And I remember when they put her on my belly, and your hand was on her too. I looked at her and I thought…"

"What?"

"I thought," she said quietly, "look what we have. Not you and me," she tried to explain. "Her and me. I thought, look at this, baby girl. Look at this man we've got. Look at the dad I gave you. Aren't we the lucky women."

"Aw, sweetheart," he said, not sounding sleepy anymore.

"And you know what?"

"No, what?"

She turned around to face him, felt him holding her, and knew it was true. Eleven years and three more babies later, it was still true. She put a soft hand on his jaw, there in the dark, and told him. "I still think so."

the harder they fall

♡

Nic followed Emma into his parents' tidy brick house. A light left on outside for them, more lights still on in the lounge. His parents were still up, then, because his dad would never have left a light on in an empty room.

Despite his best intentions, he felt the tension rising, drawing his muscles taut. His mum and dad were normally in bed by ten sharp, and it was…he glanced at his watch. Nearly ten-thirty.

His mum wasn't there. Just his dad. On the couch, watching a replay of the latest IPL match on the big-screen TV set against the wall. His stockinged feet on the coffee table, and baby George sprawled over his chest, sound asleep.

"Hi, Dad," Nic said warily. "What happened?"

"Shh." George Senior glared at him. "You'll wake him."

"Nah," Nic said. "We won't. Sleeps like a rock, once he's gone off. What happened?"

"Keep your voice down, at least," George growled. "Took me ages to settle him down. He cried, didn't want his granny." His hand went to the baby's back, gave it a rub. "Stubborn little bugger."

"Wonder where he gets that," Nic muttered as Emma bent down to retrieve George, who indeed barely stirred, and carry him off to his cot.

For some reason, and to Nic's utter astonishment, the baby preferred his grandpa. And against all odds, after a lifetime of cantankerousness that hadn't showed noticeable signs of easing up anywhere else, the adoration was mutual.

Nic's mum had always told him his dad had a soft side. It had only taken about thirty years for Nic to see it.

Emma came back into the room. "Everybody happily asleep," she said, settling onto the loveseat, and Nic sat down beside her for the report. "Did Ellen go to bed, George?"

He grunted. "Yeh. No sense in both of us being kept up."

Nic opened his mouth to tell his dad that he could have put George back down again, that it wouldn't have taken him much time at all to fall asleep on his own, but Emma laid a hand over his, and he shut it again.

"How did Zack and Harry do?" Emma asked.

"Had their tea, then Zack had to take Harry out and show him his new sandbox." The one his dad had built this spring as a surprise for his grandsons. "Made a proper mess of themselves, had to have another bath afterwards."

"Because Zack loves it," Emma said. "That was such a good idea of yours."

Laying it on a bit thick, Nic thought, but George grunted again, and Nic could tell it was a happy grunt. If there was such a thing.

"Your mum got your old soldiers out of the cupboard," he told Nic. "Yours and Dan's. Did you know she'd saved those?"

"No." Nic laughed. "Our GI Joes? I'd have thought they'd have gone to some op shop yonks ago. She saved them?"

"Forgotten them until just recently, when she was having a clean-out," George said. "Saving them up for an occasion ever since, and she thought this was it. Got the soldiers and the trucks and all. Even the tank I got you that Christmas. The tank wasn't running, of course, but I cleaned off the connections, put a new battery in, and she was good as gold. Boys loved that. Making the gun spin around and all. Had quite the battle in there."

"I hope you were careful with the baby," Nic said. "He's putting everything in his mouth these days. And those soldiers have some small parts, don't they. He could bite something off, choke on it."

His father glared at him. "Think I'd be that careless with my grandson? D'you imagine you're the only man in the world who's ever been a dad? I'm a wee bit smarter than that, I hope. Did you or Dan ever choke on a toy?"

"Well, not that I remember," Nic admitted.

Another grunt. "Too right you didn't. Because I wouldn't've let you. Anyway, we didn't let the baby in the sandbox, of course. Past his bedtime, wasn't it. Course, I had to put him down, too," he added with a sigh. "But never mind."

Nic held it in, said goodnight, took a quick peek at the kids.

Zack and Harry, sleeping peacefully in the twin beds in Dan's old room, clearly worn out with their exciting day. And George in his cot, his thick, curly brown hair going in all directions, his thumb in his mouth. Lying in his favorite position, knees beneath him, bum in the air, in the All Black pajamas Zack had insisted his baby brother needed.

Nic smiled at the sight, tucked the blanket more securely around him, then left the room, closed the door softly behind him, and walked down the hall to the bedroom next door.

Emma was pulling her nightdress out of the closet. She turned at his entrance, looked at his face, and started to giggle.

He couldn't help it. He laughed. She giggled some more, and he was laughing so hard he was gasping, trying to be quiet so his dad wouldn't hear, falling across the bed and pulling Emma with him.

"The tougher they are," she said at last, wiping her face on his T-shirt, the way she'd done so many times before, "the harder they fall."

a bit caveman

♡

Everyone had left, finally. Drew had thought they'd never go. He'd been afraid Hannah would get too tired again, and he didn't want her too tired. Not for her, and not for him.

Now, he stood with her in front of the wall-to-wall mirror in the expansive white and gray bathroom, watched her patting her face dry beside him with a white hand towel, then pulling the pins out of the knot at the back of her head until the heavy plait fell down her back.

He set his toothbrush back in the rack, turned and leaned a hip against the tile edge, and looked at her.

"Take it down for me," he said. "Out of the plait."

Her blue eyes, always so innocent in her pretty face, flew to his in the mirror. He saw them widen, search his own. And then her hands were going slowly to the white-blonde plait, pulling it in front of her body so it hung to her hip, beginning to untwist it so the curling tendrils fell free around her body.

And just like that. Just like that. Just her eyes, and her hair.

She was still looking at him, her lips parted a bit now, that Cupid's bow on her top lip that still did him in. He'd longed to trace it with his tongue the very first day he'd met her, and he still did.

She could tell, too, because he could hear her breath coming harder just from this. Just from those few words, from his gaze on her. The knowledge that he had that much power over her...it was a thrill, still. Always.

Her hands reached the top of the thick plait. She loosened the final twist, lifted the heavy fall of hair in both hands, shook it loose around her, and he stood there and watched her do it.

Just watching, nothing more, and he was falling fast. Maybe he wasn't the one with the power after all.

He picked up the extra-large tub of rich mango-papaya moisturizing cream she smoothed religiously onto every centimeter of herself every night to keep her pale skin supple, especially as her pregnancy advanced. He loved the smell of that stuff, the silkiness of her skin. Time to show her how much.

"Take off your nightgown, sweetheart," he told her. "Because I think you need somebody to do this for you tonight."

"Drew." Her chest was rising and falling noticeably now with every breath, and they hadn't even started. "I'm not...you don't want to look that closely." She laughed a little. "I know you don't."

He saw the uncertainty in her face, and his heart twisted. Finn had been right, and he was going to do something about that. He was going to convince her, or he was going to die trying.

"Don't you know," he asked her, "how sexy you are to me right now? Come on. Take it off for me. Show me your beautiful body. Please."

She looked at him again, then, so slowly, obeyed, and he let out a breath he hadn't realized he'd been holding. The white cotton rode up her body, over her head, and he reached a hand out, ran it over the perfectly rounded contour of her bare belly, the skin smooth and shining as marble, then over a full breast as it lifted to fill his hand. Her arms were over her head, and her pale skin was so translucent, he could see every blue vein outlined beneath the surface as if it had been etched by a sculptor.

So pretty. So vulnerable. He wanted to protect her, and at the same time...not. He wanted to feel her giving him all that sweet vulnerability, to feel himself taking it. He moved his hand, felt the sensitive tip hardening under his palm, heard the hitch in her breath, and that was all it took. He was gone.

"Undies," he said, his mouth dry, and she dropped the nightgown to the carpet, pulled those down too, kicked them aside.

"Bed, don't you think?" he asked. Not that he needed to go anywhere. Here would have worked brilliantly for him, the way he felt right now. But rushing her was wrong, especially now. He'd take his time, show her how much he loved it. She needed to know it, and he needed it too.

"And candles, I think," he added. "Because I love to look at you in the candlelight. And I want to see you tonight."

She laughed, just a breath, turned and walked into the bedroom, the blinds on the tall windows closed now against the soft summer night, but the windows open, a sigh of sea air coming through.

He could tell by the way she carried herself that she was believing, now. That she knew how excited he was, and that she was feeling the same way. The urgency pulled at him again, the anticipation of what was to come almost as sweet as the reality would be. Almost. Because it had been a while, as tired as she'd been, and it would be another long wait as soon as the baby came. He was going to make this one count.

She pulled the white duvet back, lay down, and waited for him. Because she always did.

He reached in the drawer for the box of matches, struck one and touched it to the wick of the heavy white pillar candle on the table, and then, when it had flared into life, came around the bed and did the same on her side. Touched the light switch with a finger, and then it was just Hannah and the bed, lit by the soft, flickering golden glow of candlelight.

He hadn't just been talking. She was beautiful. And he wanted her.

He pulled his T-shirt over his head, emerged from it to find her pushing herself up to sit, shoving his boxer briefs down his legs. Her hand was reaching for him, stroking, her touch at once soft and burning as hot as the flames he'd just ignited.

And then she bent, kissed him where he needed it most, and every bit of his attention was there. Right there, right now, and this wasn't what he'd planned. Not at all.

"First." She looked up at him and smiled a little, all of her so soft and sweet. "First. Present for my nap."

"Ah…" His tongue felt clumsy in his mouth. "I want to make you feel good. To show you."

"And you will." She'd risen to her feet, was pushing him to sit on the edge of the bed in her place. "You're going to show me everything. But first, I'm going to show you."

She was standing between his thighs, her hands on his shoulders, stroking down the heavy muscle of his upper arms, lingering a bit, then moving onto his chest to explore him there, and he knew she loved what she was feeling, and loved knowing it.

She knew exactly what he liked, all his most sensitive spots, her clever fingers teasing out a response his body was all too eager to give. And then she turned her hands, grazed the skin of his sides with her fingernails, a long, slow caress, down and down, and he could feel the goose-flesh form.

"Want a pregnant wife on her knees for you?" she asked him, her fingers trailing over his abdomen now, so close. So close. Her voice was so soft he could barely hear it, because she was shy, always, about talking in bed. Which only made it hotter when she did. "Would that be a good thing?"

"Yeh," he managed to get out. He put out a hand to support her as she lowered herself, and thought he was going to explode right then and there.

He didn't, because she took her time. She took it slowly, as if she knew that was what he needed.

He'd wanted to please her tonight, to make her feel pretty, to make her feel desired. Instead, he was wrapping his hands through pale strands of hair, twisting his fists in it, closing his eyes and opening them again, because he couldn't stand not to watch her like this.

And if there was ever a sight to make a man feel powerful, surely it was this. The sight of her naked and pregnant, her beautiful hair streaming around her, one hand on his broad thigh, the other one helping out her pretty mouth. And that mouth working so hard. His wife on her knees, her only desire to please him. Willing to do whatever he wanted. Whatever he needed.

His breath was rasping in his throat, and he was shifting on the bed, his muscles tightening. He was getting much too close, and this wasn't how he wanted to end it. He wanted more. He wanted everything.

He pulled her back from him by the hair, as gently as he could manage it.

"Hannah," he said, his voice coming out rough. "Wait. I need more."

She looked up at him, licked her lips, and he almost lost it.

"Geez," he groaned. "I need to…"

She didn't answer. Instead, she turned around, still on her knees, and dropped to her hands.

And there she was. Almost the only position that worked, this far along, and his favorite, and he was nothing but burning now. He was there behind her, his hand diving between her legs, feeling the sweet slickness there, how close she was already, as if what she'd done to him, she'd felt herself.

"So good," he told her, rubbing a little harder, seeing her start to squirm, hearing the panting gasps turning to moans, feeling her on the brink. He kept on, got another hand around her, found a heavy breast and began to caress her there as well. Gentle pressure, teasing the sensitive flesh, keeping up the swift strokes with his other hand, and feeling what the extra sensation did to her. Delaying the moment when he would be inside her, because he wanted to be there for it, to feel her orgasm around him, and her contractions were so strong when she was this far along. So powerful, and so good.

"Come on, sweetheart," he told her. "Come on."

"Drew," she gasped. "Please. Please."

"Not until you're coming." If his voice was rough, he took care that his hands weren't. "Come on, Hannah. Let me feel it."

He was over her, around her, and she was rocking hard into his hand, nothing gentle at all about the wave taking her up. She was falling, plunging, crying out, and he was guiding himself inside her, feeling her grip him so tightly as the spasms continued, again and again, in a long, rolling, powerful orgasm that took him along for the ride.

He groaned, felt himself going fast. She had a hand back where his had been, as if she couldn't help herself, and she was still keening, and he could swear she was going to come again. Or still, because the contractions had barely eased before they were grabbing him again, pulling him down with her until his panting breath, her soft cries were equaled by the roaring in his head, and he was being dragged down, tumbling over the edge with her.

Drowned. Shattered. Gone.

He slowed at last, sank his head to her back and rested it there, breathed for a moment. He felt her trembling beneath him and rolled to his back, pulled her gently down with him onto the plush cream pile of the carpet.

"That wasn't…" he got out, "at *all* how I meant this to go. I had a whole romantic…plan. Been thinking about it all day."

She hummed a little and nuzzled his neck, which felt just as good as everything else she'd done. He ran a hand over her hip, down her thigh, felt the press of her belly against his side, the ripple that was their son moving inside her, and smiled with pure contentment.

"Come on," he said, getting to his feet and pulling her up with him. "Come lie down for me. Let's get you on this bed. We'll pretend this is the beginning, and I'll show you what I meant to do."

♡

"Drew..." she managed. She couldn't even stand up. She was leaning against him a little, limp and boneless, the body that had felt so ungainly earlier that day thrumming with satisfaction. "I'm fine. I'm *so* fine."

"Nah." He picked up her jar of body butter. "Lie on down, now, because you didn't get a chance to put this on yourself tonight, and it's my turn anyway."

He cleaned her up first, and she lay back, her upper body propped up by the pillows he arranged for her, and let him do it, because she'd have let him do just about anything. Then he was straddling her, sitting below her belly, scooping out handfuls of rich body butter and rubbing it into her arms, her chest.

She had to smile at the time he took over her breasts. "Mmm," she said. "You're so...concerned."

"Yeh," he said, his touch gentle, but so deliciously male, the roughness of his hand a thrilling contrast to the smooth coolness of the cream. "No point in doing a job at all if you're not prepared to get stuck in and do it right. And you know I always get stuck in. Planning to do it right, too. Planning to get you noisy again tonight."

His words stoked the flame again, and she moaned a little, saw the satisfied smile forming on his face.

"That's right," he told her, his hands, his fingers still working, because he knew exactly how to touch her, how sensitive her breasts were, and he loved giving her pleasure there. "Just like that. I want you loud. Going to take care that you are."

He shifted off her at last to give her legs the same loving attention, and by the time he was smoothing the butter onto her inner thighs, stroking higher and higher, she was breathing hard.

"Feels good, doesn't it?" he said huskily.

"Yes," she sighed, closing her eyes to focus on the sensation.

"Same for me," he told her. "Your hands on me feel so much better than mine. I think that every time I'm away from you. I close my eyes, pretend that's your hand, your mouth there. That I'm inside you. Tell myself I'll be there soon, imagine what it'll be like, what I'll do. When I get off the bus, off the plane...I'm that much closer. But not as close as I mean to be. Not as close as I need to be."

She didn't answer. She was watching him now, his familiar, beloved face tough, intent, the way she'd seen it so often. But this time, all that fierce concentration was for her.

He shifted to her belly, his hands stroking its contours as he smoothed the rich cream into her skin.

"So pretty," he told her. "Always. You have the most beautiful skin. Thought so that first time, when I had you on my boat. Wanted to touch it just like this. Wanted to kiss it. Wanted to lay you down and...touch you."

She knew what he'd wanted to do, what he wasn't saying, and the thrill of it shivered along her skin along with his hands. She reached a hand up, traced the network of fine white lines above his eyebrow, along his jawline, his chin. Scarred, battle-hardened. A warrior, first and last. All man, and all hers.

"I wanted to touch you too," she told him softly. "So much. You...overwhelmed me. You still do. And what you said, about how you feel..."

She stopped, watched him twist the top on the tub of cream, set it on the table, then slide back over her, all the way down so his big hands cupped either side of her belly. Her breath hitched as he kissed her there, below her navel, began to move down, his hands stroking the skin of her abdomen, making her feel beautiful, and desired, and his.

"When you're...gone, and you imagine me," she managed to say, "that it's my hand, and my mouth. I...I imagine you too, those nights. When I..." She stopped on a gasp as his mouth found her, as his lips and tongue began to work. "But it never feels like...this," she got out. "Like...oh." He'd found exactly the right spot, and she could barely speak. "Like...you."

She wouldn't have thought she could manage it again, or that she needed to. But she could, and she did. She needed it so much. His gentle touch, and, later, when it wasn't quite as gentle, when his mouth, his hands were harder, more urgent. When her own hands were fisting, yanking frantically at the sheet beneath her, and then, in desperation, grabbing for his hair, and she was pulling it, just like he'd pulled hers.

He took that for the signal it was, increased the pressure until she was rising off the bed, crying out her pleasure, knowing he was feeling it as surely as she'd felt his. Knowing that he needed to know he was giving it to her. That her pleasure was his own. Always.

♡

She was still trembling when he rose up over her again, pulled one of the pillows out from under her and stuck it beneath his own head, settled down beside her.

"I should put my nightgown on," she murmured, snuggling closer, the heat of his big body radiating through her. Knowing that he knew she really meant, "Please go get me my nightgown," and that he would do it.

Except that he didn't.

"Not tonight," he said, stroking a hand down her back, soothing her as if she'd been a skittish horse, and she sighed and let him do it. "Please. I love you naked. Love to touch you, feel your skin against mine."

"Even when I'm this pregnant?" She searched his face. "It wouldn't be better to cover up a bit?"

She could see the amusement crinkling the corners of his gray eyes. As cold and forbidding as the winter sea when they needed to be, but so warm when he looked at her.

"After all this," he said, "you can still ask me that? You really don't know?"

"Know what?" His hand was still moving, sending wonderful tingles through her.

"How much I want you when you're like this. Why I do."

When she didn't answer, just continued to look at him, he went on. "It's a...it's a male thing, I guess. Well," he said, chuckling a bit, "it'd have to be, wouldn't it? It's... how much you're mine, when you're pregnant. I see you like that, my baby in your belly, and it's...it's possession, I reckon. Virility. Proof. Something like that. It's your body showing the world what I did, what I did to you. And I know that's a bit caveman," he hurried on. "But then, I *am* a bit cavemen. I can be. I know."

He had his hand on the side of her distended abdomen now, a soft touch over the firm contours. "It's all mine," he confessed, "and I love it. And the more you feel that way to me, the more I want you."

She was tingling from more than his touch now. "Then I guess I'm a cavewoman myself," she told him, "because that's exactly how it feels to me too. That I'm yours, and how much I want to be. And the thing that turns me on the most, so *you* know? It's knowing you want me. Having you tell me so, seeing it in your eyes, feeling it in your body. That's the sexiest thing you can do for me. Just want me that much. Just show me you do."

"If that's all it takes," he said, "I'm a lucky man, not that I don't know that already. I want you, and I can show you how much I do. How often I do. Which is at least as often as you want it. And exactly that much, too. More than that much."

She smiled at him, loving him so hard her heart ached with it, because she knew what he was doing. What he was doing for her.

"Thank you," she said, her voice nearly a whisper.

He laughed a little, leaned over, and kissed her hair. "Nah, sweetheart. Thank *you.*"

morning light

♡

Hannah woke to more bright morning light around the blinds. She wasn't alone this time, she realized. Drew's quiet approach through the double doors of the master bedroom must have woken her.

He came across to the bed, a mug in his hand, and set it on the table beside her. She scooted over, patted the spot next to her, and hoisted herself up.

A smile, and he was sitting down, reaching a hand out for the hair that had never made it back into its braid the night before, smoothing it back from her face. And looking at her like that was exactly what he wanted to do. Look.

Not just at her face, either. He gazed at her bare shoulders and breasts for a long moment, then asked, clearing his throat, "Uh...want your nightdress? Or are you just showing me some of my favorite things again? Is this a message? Because if it is, I'm happy to get it."

"Both," she said with a happy smile at his response. "Showing you, if they're still your favorites. I hope they are. And yes, please."

He got up, went to the chair where he'd obviously laid it when he'd got up this morning. He was dressed already, of course—navy blue shorts and a gray T-shirt, his feet bare. Country casual. Tauranga style.

He helped her into the white nightdress, sat down beside her again, and she settled back, picked up her mug, and took a sip of herbal tea. Smiled at him some more, and enjoyed the sight of him smiling back.

"Lazy again," she said. "The kids up?"

"Yeh. Mum and Dad have got them, no worries. And lazy?" He laughed. "Nah. You earned it."

"I did, didn't I?" She pulled her hair back, preened a little under his appreciative gaze. "How do you manage to make a woman who's almost nine months pregnant feel this sexy?"

"Maybe by thinking she is?" he suggested.

"Guess that's it." She was smiling like a fool, but that's how she felt. "Better not share that one in my next interview, or everybody will *really* be jealous."

He laughed. "Nah. Just clue them in on my more disgusting habits, make them think that fella they're waking up next to is a bargain in comparison."

"Oh, yeah. They'll buy that."

"But what I came up to ask you," he said, "is this. Mako was thinking we should take you girls to see a movie this afternoon. Get the grandparents babysitting again, since they aren't complaining so far."

"Everybody?"

"Well, yeh. Anybody who wants to go. Another beach day would be too much for you and Kristen, we thought, and a movie might be a good distraction for the two of you anyway. Going to be a hot one again today, and the cinema's got that lovely air con. I know that wouldn't come amiss. Sound good? Or too much social time? Had enough?"

"No," she said. "That does sound good. Better than staying at home. Distraction, like you said." She tried to pull herself up a little more, a groan escaping despite herself.

"What is it?" he asked.

"Just my back," she admitted. "A little achy this morning, that's all." A lot achy, in fact, but she hated complaining about physical ailments to Drew. How could you whine about your aching back to a man who'd played entire rugby games with broken bones? "You barely feel it at the time," he'd tried to explain, but she hadn't really taken his word for it.

"Roll over," he said now.

"No, that's OK. I'm fine."

"Nah," he said. "Least I can do. Who knows, that may have been from me. Not sure your back was helped by having a hundred-ten kilos of me on it last night."

He was rolling her onto her side as he spoke, his hands finding the spot at the small of her back that always gave her trouble. The massage offered instant relief, and she sighed and relaxed into it.

"You weren't on it," she said as best she could against the sheet beneath her cheek, the pressure of his strong hands. "You were over it. And I liked that just fine."

"I liked it too," he promised, the satisfaction in his voice letting her know how much he meant it. "So what d'you think? Movie? Or you could stay here, have a rest, since we'll have the wedding tomorrow. Yet another event. Mum and Dad could take the kids to the beach," he added, forestalling her objections. "Nobody'd bat an eye, you know that."

"No," she said. "I'd like to go. As long as the movie doesn't have too many explosions. Violence when I'm pregnant…I hate it. Must be some instinctive thing. Some maternal thing."

He laughed, his hands keeping to their task. "No violence, except maybe to the boys' sensibilities. Mako found a rom-com. Says he'll enjoy it too, though that may be taking it a bit far."

She laughed a little herself at that. "Maybe he's in touch with his feminine side."

"That's what he says. That he gets enough violence on the paddock, doesn't need it anywhere else in his life. But I have my doubts. I don't think boys ever get tired of watching things blow up."

"I know Jack doesn't." She was feeling a little sleepy again under his ministrations, her eyes closing, because that felt good.

"Or could be Mako just knows how to keep a Montgomery girl happy," Drew said. "Though I warn you, I'm not quite willing to go that far. I'll take you. But I won't promise to enjoy it."

"Someday, you know," she told him with a sigh, "you're going to get tired of being so perfect. I'm going to find out that there's a Mr. Hyde somewhere, out doing all the things you don't. Saying all the things you've never said to me. I know those things must be bottled up somewhere."

"Nah," he said, sounding, as always, so completely sure. "Or if I do, you've got a Mrs. Hyde somewhere yourself. Turnabout's fair play, that's all. I seem to remember somebody who was pretty good to me after I hung up my boots. For quite a long time, because it was a fair few months there before I came right."

"You still weren't…nasty," she objected. "You didn't do anything wrong. All you did was go quiet. And go fishing."

"Yeh. Left you and Jack to do it every time, too, even though you were pregnant. And did you give me a hard time about that?"

"Of course not. It was tough. I knew it was tough."

"You did. But most women would've pouted that I wasn't spending more time with them, badgered me to talk about my feelings. I don't like to talk about my feelings."

"Huh." She couldn't help teasing a little. "You astonish me."

He laughed. "Yeh. Guess that's obvious."

"Just because you don't talk about them," she said, "doesn't mean you don't have them. Or that I don't see them."

"Exactly," he said with satisfaction. "How's that, on the back? Better?"

She rolled, tested it out. "Much better."

In fact, the achiness remained, a low, dull reminder, but there was no help for that. If Drew could play rugby with a broken jaw, she could get through a day with an aching back. That was life.

meaning it

♡

Hugh got out of the car with Josie, reached into the back seat for the plastic container of tuatua and pumpkin fritters she'd insisted on bringing along.

"They had everyone to dinner last night," she'd told him, "and now they're having us all again for lunch today? If Hannah's willing to do it, I'm not coming empty-handed. Besides, give me something to do, and a use for some of these tuatua that the kids and I collected this morning."

"I thought they were for tomorrow."

"Yeh, well, we may have got a bit carried away."

"Most women don't spend the time before their weddings fishing," he pointed out. "Or gathering clams. Not to mention cooking."

"Maybe Maori women do, you thought of that? Could be you've just known the wrong women."

"Well, I know that's true. But I still doubt it, on the fishing."

"Fishing was yesterday. Just doing my bit, staying involved, trying to keep myself from getting stage fright. Would you rather have a Bridezilla, throwing a wobbly because I gained two kilos and my dress doesn't fit?"

"Nah. Keep fishing," he said hastily. "And *did* you gain two kilos?"

"Of course not," she said, because of course not. She never did. She couldn't afford to. "But I'm glad to stay busy. Otherwise, who knows."

So here they were in Hannah and Drew's big kitchen, reheating Josie's fritters while the rest of the group came and went, setting up their impromptu picnic on the tables outside before their movie date.

"Why do I get the feeling," Hugh asked Josie in a low voice, flipping a luscious orange fritter in the hot pan, "that we're the only two people here who didn't get lucky last night? Some serious touching going on out there. I know that look." A hand on a back, a quick kiss, a secret smile, even the occasional grope. For everybody but him, and he was the groom.

Josie let out a startled laugh. "Shh. Maybe they're just relaxed."

He snorted. "I've been that relaxed too. Pity I can hardly remember it."

"You just wait," she promised.

He sighed. "That's what you said last night. Feel like a kid waiting for Christmas. Got that big, beautiful present sitting there, just taunting me. Wishing I could unwrap it right now. Knowing I have to wait, and so sure that I can't. Wondering if I could get up in the night and sneak a peek. Maybe even take it out of the box and play with it a little." He had his arm around her now, his lips at her neck.

She reached over, shoved her spatula under the smoking fritters in his pan, opened the wall oven, and slid them onto the platter. "Those are yours," she informed him. "You'll recognize them. They're the black ones." She transferred a couple more of the golden disks into both their pans. "You're relieved of duty, mister. You're too distracted to cook."

Which was nothing but true, and had been for days, and it was only getting worse. And it wasn't the wedding.

They'd gone for a walk after dinner the night before, when Josie had stood to do the washing-up after dinner and Hugh had risen to help her, and Josie's mum had waved them off.

"Amelia and Charlie will do it," she told them. "Take this boy up the bush track, Josie. I think he needs an outing."

"Makes me sound like a dog," he said.

Arama snorted a bit at that. "You saying you don't want to go for a walk with Josie?"

"Nah," he said with a grin. "I'm not saying that."

"Then go on," she said. "Get out of here and do it."

They'd taken their walk up the mountain without talking much, the steepness of the rocky climb, the roughness of the track precluding conversation. It had been good to be alone with her all the same. It felt like ages, even though it had actually only been a few days. A few days of sleeping in the caravan with the kids, of her being in the house. Of preparations and family and friends and children. And not nearly enough Josie.

The shadows had been lengthening by the time they'd approached the house again. They could see, from their vantage point up above, the level blocks of orchards, the green of kiwifruit vines, the trees heavy with avocados and citrus. Josie's parents' farm, and all the other small farms and orchards around it, spreading in both directions. The rolling green of paddocks dotted with houses, barns, outbuildings, all of it sloping inevitably down to the little settlement of Katikati, barely visible below. The darkening mountains behind them, the sea beyond. Nothing but idyllic, a landscape straight from a postcard.

It was a sight to gladden the heart in the soft, glowing light of evening, but it hadn't entirely gladdened Hugh's. Because he could also see that Josie's family was spread around outside the house. Her brother and sister-in-law on the front patio, most of the rest of them on the deck, enjoying the evening. Getting in his way.

"Come on," he said before they got down to the drive. He opened the gate to the orchard blocks. "Last chance."

"Are we being bad?" Josie asked, widening her eyes at him. She was getting into her new role, Hugh could tell. Instead of the constant vamping of Evil Dr. Eva, he was getting the enthusiasm of Anika Luatua, rural schoolteacher. He knew which one he preferred. And if Anika didn't capture some hearts pretty quickly, Hugh would be gobsmacked, because she did the business for him. Although he didn't mind her showing him Dr. Eva from time to time, either. A command performance. That worked too.

But just now, there was no Dr. Eva in sight. Instead, she had taken off, was running down the row, between the vines, looking back at him, laughing, then ducking out of sight, and he was laughing too and chasing her. Which wasn't easy, because she fit beneath the interlocking mesh of vines, and he had to duck to avoid them. Wedding or no, if he damaged the vines, her dad would have something to say about it.

She led him up the next row, down another. Ducked across a few rows, so he had to search for her, and was halfway up when he finally caught her, slung an arm around her waist and reeled her in.

"Got you," he told her, turning her in his arms. "Not getting away from me that easily. Now that I've caught you, I'm holding onto you, remember?"

Her spectacular chest was heaving with effort, her dark eyes sparkling with fun, and bloody hell, but she was beautiful. No makeup, shorts and T-shirt and boots, her long dark hair in a ponytail. Beautiful.

"Should've guessed I couldn't run away from you," she said, her gorgeous mouth curved in a laugh.

"My job, isn't it," he said huskily. "Chasing people down. Taking what I want."

Her eyes widened with some more of that innocent alarm. "Should I be scared?"

He smiled. "Eventually. In about two days." He led her over to their bench, sat on the rustic wooden seat, pulled her down beside him, and took her in his arms. "For right now, though," he told her, "you should just get ready to be kissed pretty hard."

He did kiss her, and then he kissed her some more. Did a fair amount of groping, too.

"You looked pretty good in that red bikini today," he said, his mouth at her neck, his hand on a luscious breast that fit it perfectly, that seemed like it had been made for him to hold, and that he hadn't touched in much too long. "Bringing that one on the honeymoon?"

"Mmm," she said, sighing and shifting a bit on the bench. "Thought you'd like that. That's one of them I'm bringing. The other one's even better."

"Don't see how that's even possible." His hand was up under the hem of the T-shirt now, moving inside her bra and finding warm flesh, making her squirm a bit, and making him heat up at the silk of her beneath his palm.

And that most wonderful spot. The nipple pebbling under his touch, her gasp as he played with it.

"Smaller, I mean," she got out. "The bikini."

"And again..." he said, moving his hand just to see her eyes darken, her mouth open.

"You ever heard of a...thong?" she asked.

He groaned. "You're going to kill me. And now I understand," he went on, keeping his hand moving, keeping her going, feeling her respond to him, "why they used to have that rule about not being with the bride before the wedding. The fella might still have cold feet, but every other part of him would be dying to get that ceremony done. Don't know if I'm going to make it."

He bent to kiss her again. "Rough sex on a bench," he whispered in her ear, and felt her shudder. "How does that sound?"

"Splinters," she said with a gasp.

"Not so rough, then. You on top of me. I'll make it good. Promise." Was she going to go for it? Bloody hell, he hoped so.

"No," she sighed. "Wouldn't put it past my dad to take a walk out here. Nah. You wait, boy." She pulled away from him, smoothed her hair a bit, let him know that playtime was over. "*Do* you have cold feet?"

"No." He pulled her shirt down with regret, because the thought of sitting here, with her on top of him, his hands on her hips, shoving her down over him, again and again...he could've done that. He'd been about two seconds away from doing that, if her feet hadn't been colder than his. "My feet, and every other part of me, too, are nothing but hot for you. But hang on," he realized. "Do you?" Why was she asking?

"A bit," she admitted.

He felt the shock of it, a punch to his gut, the mood changing completely with those two little words.

"What..." He swallowed. "What is it? The kids? Me? What?" He shut his mouth on the protest, the promises. Stopped, sat, and waited, his heart in his throat.

"All those pregnancies today," she said, shifting away from him even farther, looking through the gathering darkness at the vines. So fertile, like everything around them. Everything except her. "All those kids."

"Two of them were our kids," he reminded her. "And I meant what I said."

"I guess I keep wondering..." she said, and trailed off.

"What?" he asked gently, taking her hand, swallowing against the pain in her eyes. "What do you wonder?"

She looked at him. Straight and sober, nothing but honest. "Not that you'd leave. But that you'd be sorry you couldn't."

He started to tell her that they'd been through this again and again, forced himself to stop and think instead.

"Anything other than the baby you think I'll be sorry about?" he asked.

"No. At least..." She laughed a little, though it didn't seem funny to him. "Nothing my mind is torturing me with. Nothing but that."

"Then how about if we make a plan?" he asked, keeping her hand in his, trying to show her that he had her, that he was holding her. "First thing we do when we're back, after the honeymoon. Check into what it takes to adopt a baby. Decide when the soonest is that we'll be ready to do it. Whether that's now, or a bit later. Fill out whatever we have to fill out, anyway, to say why we'd be the best. Get started."

He did his best to smile, put a hand up to her cheek, held her there. "Because, sweetheart. Any mum who has to give her baby up? Any girl facing that choice—why wouldn't she choose you? I know she couldn't do better. I know how lucky that baby would be."

Her expressive brown eyes were brimming with tears. One of them escaped, slid down her face, and he brushed it away with his thumb.

"So if that's it," he went on gently, "we can do that. I'll be right there with you. We'll do it together. And you'll have your baby."

She was crying now. Too much for any thumb to wipe away, so he held her against him instead, let her let it out, let it go. All the tension, all the worry he hadn't known she was carrying.

"But there's one thing," he said against her hair. "When you're worried like this, you need to let me know, let me help you carry it. Whatever it is. I'm a pretty clueless fella. I may need some help to catch on. But once you tell me, I'll be there. I promise."

She pulled back, her hands on his shoulders, her eyes swimming with tears, but steady on his again. "You really mean it," she said. "You'll really do it."

"I'll do anything it takes," he promised her. "Anything at all. I'm going to stand in that church day after tomorrow. I'm going to hold your hand. And when the man asks me the question? I'm going to say I will. And I'm going to mean it."

quite the interruption

♡

That had done the business. And it was even true.

And today, they were going to the movies with all those pregnant women. But then, Josie's sister-in-law was pregnant too, and a couple of the cousins as well. There really was no escape, and he could see what she had been living with these past years.

Well, the movie was a bit of an escape, at least. For her, and for him. Nothing but fluff, a Christmas-themed rom-com. All courtship, and not a baby in sight. Snow and dark and cold and all the things New Zealand wasn't, although the thoroughly air-conditioned chill of the multiplex was doing its best to set the tone.

Hugh was sitting at the far end of the group. And holding Josie's hand, because if holding her hand was all there was, he was holding her hand. He wouldn't put it past himself to steal a kiss or two before the lights went up.

He wasn't thinking about that just now, though. Because the fella on the screen who'd left the girl behind at the airport to take the new job had just turned around in the boarding queue, was running back through the crowd, dodging around passengers, leaving his luggage and the new post and the new life behind. The music was swelling, and bloody hell, but Hugh was misting up himself.

It must be the wedding. He hadn't cried when the All Blacks had won the Championship back in October, when Nate had hoisted the trophy overhead. He'd been happy, of course he had. He'd been bloody rapt about it. He'd laughed. He might even, if the truth were screwed out of him, have choked up a bit. But he hadn't cried.

He hadn't cried when the whistle had blown on a victorious Northern tour, either, on the team's resurgence after their shocker season of the year before, at knowing they were taking their rightful place again as the powerhouse of world rugby. At knowing they were back, that they were stronger than ever for the losses. That they were, above all, a team.

No, he hadn't cried during any of those. He hadn't even cried when he'd come home to Josie and the kids. He'd wanted to, but he hadn't.

But like it or not, that was a tear making its warm, wet way down his cheek. He didn't dare brush it away, because Josie would notice, he knew it. He needed to sniff a bit, too, and he wasn't doing that either.

He didn't even want to think about what would happen during the wedding. Every time he thought about her walking down the aisle to him...

His thoughts were interrupted by some commotion down the aisle. He looked over, saw the seats banging up as the others filed out. He looked up at the screen. The fella was still running. What?

"Something's happened," Josie whispered to him, tugging at his hand. "Come on."

The other patrons in the theater were shifting, muttering at the disruption, and Hugh ducked as low as he could from his considerable height, followed Josie down the empty row to the end, nearly slipping on a puddle on the concrete floor along the way. Somebody'd spilled their drink.

They made it up the aisle, into the carpeted lobby, and there the others were. Standing in a little circle around Hannah, who had Drew's arm around her, and was looking embarrassed and uncomfortable. Physically or otherwise, Hugh couldn't tell.

"Gone into labor," Reka told Josie.

"Sorry," Hannah said. "You all should go watch the end of the movie. I'm fine. If Drew just…" She stopped, her face tightening, and she looked more than uncomfortable now, was leaning into Drew, and he had his other arm around her.

"Right. Sitting down," Drew said. He looked around, but there wasn't really anyplace to sit, not up here.

"Food court," Reka said briskly. "Downstairs."

"Just a…minute," Hannah got out. "Can't…right now."

They all waited it out, and Finn was looking at his watch, a frown making his craggy features look even more forbidding than usual. Then he was looking at Jenna, and she was looking back at him.

"Fifty-six seconds," he said quietly, and if that meant anything, Hugh didn't know what it was.

Hannah gradually straightened, took a deep breath, tried to smile. "Sorry. I think…the hospital, Drew."

"Yeh," he said. "Of course. Straight away. Downstairs, first. Can you walk?"

"Of course I can. But…" She looked embarrassed. "I'm…wet. The seat. The theater. We should say something."

Hugh was confused. What? He never knew what was going on.

"Her water," Josie said quietly next to him. "Her water broke. Why her dress is wet."

"Oh." He'd heard of that, vaguely. Hadn't sounded like anything he wanted to know about, so he'd passed it right on by.

Drew didn't even respond to Hannah's concern. "Downstairs," he said, putting an arm around her and beginning to lead her toward the escalator.

"But...somebody needs to tell them," Hannah said, resisting his efforts, forcing him to stop.

"Hannah," he sighed. "It doesn't matter. They'll cope."

"It does." She actually looked distressed now. "It's such a *mess.* It's so...so *embarrassing.* It's like I...peed on the seat." She was very nearly crying, Hugh saw.

"And d'you imagine no kid has ever done that?" Drew demanded. "Come on."

"I'll tell them," Reka put in hastily when Hannah looked even more upset. "Hemi and I'll go tell them straight away, then come find you."

"Tell them the row," Hannah said, then began to stiffen again, her breath hitching.

Finn was still looking at his watch. "Three minutes," he told Drew. "Don't hang about, mate. Get her downstairs."

Drew nodded, Reka and Hemi took themselves off in the direction of the box office, and the rest of them began to follow Drew and Hannah.

She took a few steps, then stopped, leaned against Drew's chest, held onto his shoulders, breathing hard.

He waited again, his arms around her, then, as she straightened, led her onto the nearly empty "down" escalator. The "up" one held a scattering of patrons arriving for the next film, and the group attracted some curious stares. And then came the whispering, the inevitable camera phones.

Drew paid them no attention, just strode off the escalator, still holding onto Hannah. "My car's blocks away." He glanced around the group, his gaze settling on Koti. "You're the fastest," he said, pulling out his keys. "Go get it. A few blocks down Totara Street, on your right."

"No," Koti said, and Drew looked startled, as well he might. "Mine's closer. I'll get it, and I'll drive."

He didn't wait for an answer, just took off, big body graceful as always, dodging the other patrons as if he were shedding tacklers.

"I'll go out and watch for him," Finn decided. "Come tell you when he brings the car up. We can't have him looking for parking."

"Oh, man, this is embarrassing," Hannah moaned.

Of course it would be, for somebody as private as Hannah. That was easy even for Hugh to see. The presence of the group hadn't gone unnoticed. In fact, the entire food court was watching at this point, at least the Kiwis amongst them. Make that about two-thirds of the food court, then. The crowd was growing all the time, cameras were out, and this was clearly the most excitement Mt. Maunganui had seen in some time.

"Yeah, Hannah," Kate said. "Why can't you go into labor in the middle of the night like a normal person?"

"I'm just giving Koti more practice," Hannah said, still embarrassed, but trying to rally. "In case."

"We're not planning on doing it quite so dramatically," Kate said. "Ever. He fell asleep in the chair with Maia. More than twenty-four hours. I would've been glad to fall asleep myself. But as always, you're more efficient than me, Hannah."

Hannah smiled at her friend. "Always...snarky," she got out, then stiffened again, began to breathe harder, her focus clearly turning inward, and Drew uttered an exclamation, held her some more.

Hemi approached a group sitting at one of the square tables, eating Indian food from paper plates.

"Fellas," he told the young men, "we've got a bit of a situation here. I'll ask you to get up and let these ladies sit down."

The men gaped up at him for a moment. The expressions on their faces would have been comical under any other circumstances, Hugh decided.

"Yeh," one of them managed to say. "Right." They sprang to their feet, picked up their plates, and moved off fast.

Drew waited until Hannah looked more relaxed again, then set her gently into one of the plastic chairs, and Kristen and Jenna joined her in a couple of the others. At least everybody was sitting down now, and Hugh breathed a bit easier.

"Just a few minutes, sweetheart," Drew told his wife, "and we'll be on our way. No worries. But I need to call the midwife, let her know we're coming." He pulled out his phone, turned away, and was speaking into it within seconds, his voice urgent.

Hannah laughed again. Doing her best to smooth the situation for everybody else there, as if that were possible. "It's like a sitcom," she said.

"It'd only be a sitcom if Kristen and Jenna went into labor too," Kate said. She looked at Kristen, sitting beside her sister and looking sweetly concerned. "Any action?"

"No," Kristen said, clearly startled. "Of course not. I've still got more than three weeks to go."

"I have two," Hannah said, and that was another laugh, at least an attempt at one.

"Don't scare us like that, Kate," Reka said. "Bloody hell."

Drew looked up, because Finn was coming back, threading his way between the tables.

"Car's here," he said briefly, and that had been quick. But then, Koti *was* quick.

They stood to leave, but halfway to the door, Hannah sagged again. Drew gave an exclamation, swept her up in his arms, and carried her the rest of the way, the remainder of the group trailing along behind.

Koti was parked in a yellow-striped zone outside the cinema, out of the car and waiting, paying not a bit of attention to parking regulations. A crowd had formed out there too, to which Drew paid absolutely no attention. Koti had the door open, and Drew set Hannah gently into the back seat, shut her door, strode around the car and got in.

A break in the traffic, and Koti was moving off, and that was it.

"Wow," Kate said, exhaling a bit as they watched it go. "*Why* can't she have a baby without all that excitement? I'm exhausted. I just hope she's OK."

"Hospital's only twenty minutes away," Hemi said. "I don't think she's actually going to have it in the car. But it won't be long." He turned to Reka. "Don't you think?"

"Yeh," she said. "I do." She looked at Kate. "Want to go with Hemi and me to the hospital?"

"Are we going to the hospital?" Hemi asked.

"Well, yeh," Reka said. "Obviously. I'll feel better. And ring Drew's mum and dad along the way. Let them know."

"I'm coming too," Kristen said. "Liam?"

"Of course," he said. "Though I'm thinking right now that I want to drive you home."

"The hospital first, though," she said with surprise. "Don't you want to?"

He laughed a bit. "I meant, home to Welly. In fact, we might look into a hotel room next to the hospital. Because I'm terrified."

The three of them left, and Hugh and Josie were left standing on the pavement with Nic and Emma, Nate and Ally, and Finn and Jenna. The crowd around them hadn't dispersed any. In fact, it had grown.

"Well," Hugh finally said blankly, "that isn't exactly how I pictured today going. Bit of relaxation, I thought, before the wedding. Not exactly."

"Babies tend to have bad timing," Emma said. "But Hannah and Drew are both so calm and collected all the time, it's ironic that they'd be the ones to go through all that drama. You'd think they'd have better-organized babies."

"A bit exciting, always," Finn said. "No matter how well-organized the baby is. Nothing better than watching your baby be born, and nothing worse."

"Nothing *worse?*" Jenna said, staring at him.

"I mean," he hastened to say, "because you're so help-less. You can't do anything. Nothing but watch. And that's..." He exhaled. "Hard."

in the tunnel again

♡

The moment Drew jumped in on his side, he was slamming the door shut.

"Go," he told Koti, and Koti went.

"Grace Hospital," Drew added. "Go down Maunganui Road to 29. That'll be the quickest."

"Did you...call the midwife?" Hannah gasped.

"You heard me do it, sweetheart." He took her hand in his, feeling so helpless. Useless. What was he meant to do? He wanted to tell Koti to hurry, but he was already driving as quickly, as aggressively as he dared, and Drew could see it. Anyway, this was normal. Wasn't it?

"This is normal, right?" he asked. If only he'd been here for the other babies, he'd know. And he'd know what he was meant to do, too. It didn't look normal to him, because Hannah was panting now, her face strained.

It was supposed to go slower. Wasn't it? And not be this...hard, at the beginning? They'd talked about walking around in labor, in those classes. Reading. All that. Hannah didn't look like she was going to be doing any reading or walking. This must just be how it was, though, how it *really* was, and all he'd say was, men had got off way too easy.

People drove to hospital to have babies every day, though. Every single day. And every one of those women was in labor. Every one of them must look like this. But none of them was his wife.

She wasn't answering, he realized. "This is normal, right?" he asked again. "Somebody? Koti?"

He got a look back in the rear-view mirror that told him Koti didn't think it was normal at all, and his heart was hammering now.

"I don't...know," Hannah said on another gasp. "Not...really. Uhhh...Drew." She had one hand on the armrest, the other squeezing the hell out of his own hand, her fingernails digging in.

"Aw, shit." He unsnapped her seatbelt, then got behind her, pulled her against his chest and held on. He could feel the tension in her, the strain, the rock-hard belly under his palms. Her panting breath filled the car as the contraction gripped her and she struggled to breathe through it.

"How long, mate?" he asked Koti.

Koti's eyes in the mirror again. "Fifteen minutes."

It didn't sound long, and yet it sounded much too long, because the anxiety was trying to take over now, the fear clawing in his chest.

They were inching through a red light, and traffic was heavy. How could the bloody traffic be this bad, two o'clock in the afternoon in Mt. Maunganui? How the bloody hell? Tourists, who needed to get out of the way. Right now.

"Uhhh..." It was Hannah again. "I think...Oh, God, Drew. I think the baby's coming."

"Geez. Now?"

"Now," she said. "He's coming now. Oh God, Drew. I can feel it. He's coming."

He made his decision. "Pull over," he barked at Koti.

Koti glanced in the mirror again, didn't argue, just swung to the side of the road and into the first clear spot. It happened to be a bus stop, which didn't matter one bit.

"Ring 111," Drew told him. "Tell them to get here right the hell now." Because Hannah had a hand up under her dress, and the look on her face, the sound of her rapid, keening breath, the fact that there hadn't been any of those quiet minutes there were supposed to be between the contractions, had already told Drew everything he needed to know.

"We're not going to make it to the hospital, are we, sweetheart?" he asked her, shoving the fear ruthlessly down, trying to sound sure and calm. For her. "We don't have fifteen minutes, do we?"

"No," she said, and it was a sob. "Oh. Drew. I think… I think he's coming. Can you…can you do this?"

"We'll do it together," he promised, because that was what she needed to hear, and because that was what they were going to do. "We're having a baby. Good as gold."

He scooted himself out of the way as he was talking, laid her down on the seat, got the door open and stood on the pavement.

Her hands were on her belly, and she was blowing breaths out in puffs now, and that wasn't good. That was meant to happen at the end. He'd been to the class.

"What did they say?" he asked Koti, who'd got out of the car as well to stand beside him.

"Said they're coming," Koti said. "Just a few minutes. Any minute," he went on hastily.

"Right, then." Drew took a breath of his own, exhaled, worked to focus, to beat the fear back, because Hannah was doing that rapid panting again. "You got any idea what to do?"

"Yeh," Koti said, not sounding much steadier than he was himself. "Read up on it, before Maia. Just in case. Because I was nervous." He was nervous now too, it was clear.

"Then...what?" Drew asked, trying to stay patient, and it had never been harder. "What do I do?"

"You don't have to do much. Just...catch the baby. Don't pull it, don't twist anything. You sort of...support the head, when it comes out. And catch it," Koti repeated. "That's what I know. Sorry, mate. That's all I know."

Drew nodded, leaned in, because Hannah was trying to twist around, and put a gentle hand on her belly. Rock-hard again. Still.

"Get my...underwear off," she gasped. So he did. Soaked, of course. He dropped them on the floor, pushed her dress up. Modesty be damned. He needed to see.

"I'll just..." Koti said.

"Don't you dare," Drew said fiercely. "Need you here to tell me what to do. You read it, I didn't."

"Right, then." Koti blew out a long breath. "Get her closer to the...the edge. So you can get in there. Feel for the head. If it's coming."

Drew reached under her, pulled her towards him so one of her feet could brace itself against the car's side column. That helped, he could tell.

"Just going to check," he told her. He put a few gentle fingers, then his entire hand, because it fit there, inside a place that was surely wider than it was meant to stretch, but of course it had to stretch, didn't it? And felt...something, blocking his way.

"Is this it?" he asked her. "Is this him?"

"I think so," she managed to say. "Oh, Drew. I have to..."

"Tell her to pant again," Koti said beside him. "Not to push hard."

"Don't push hard," Drew told Hannah, feeling so helpless. How was she supposed to stop? It didn't seem to him that she could stop.

He was right. "I...have to," she gasped. "Ohhhh...." It was a wail, nearly a scream, and she was pushing, he could feel it.

"Put your hand over the head," Koti was saying in Drew's ear, leaning over next to him, his voice tight with urgency. "Don't let it pop out too fast."

Hannah's entire body was straining with effort, the sweat standing out on her belly, her thighs, the red blood running, and Drew swallowed. Was that normal, or was it bad? Was she in danger? He didn't know, and he'd never been more terrified, because she was screaming, the sound reverberating in his head, sending his pulse rate spiking even higher.

But there was something there now. Something dark. He put his hand over it, and it was his son. The top of his son's head. He was touching his son.

Another heave, one final scream from Hannah, trailing into a wailing cry, and the head was there, and Drew was gasping along with Hannah, along with the wrinkled, screwed-up little face emerging from her.

"One more push," he told Hannah. "He's here, sweetheart. He's almost all the way here. One more push and let him come."

He had a gentle hand under the head, because he wasn't dropping that, no matter what. Ever. He saw her gather her forces and bear down again, moaning with the pain and the effort, and there was a tiny red shoulder, and, in a gush of fluid and blood, his baby. His boy. His son.

He was here. He was born.

Drew gathered the little body in his hands as it emerged, taking care to keep a hand under his head, supporting his neck. The baby was slippery, wet, wriggling and surprisingly strong, and he'd never caught anything with more care, not in the most important game of his career. He'd never held onto anything so desperately. Because nothing had ever mattered more.

The little chest heaved, the mouth opened, and a squall came out, high, surprisingly loud, the unmistakable cry of a newborn, and it sounded so good.

"He's here," he told Hannah, his voice shaking. "He's here."

She was still lying there, gasping and crying with effort, shaking now herself, and he wished he had something to put over her, but there was nothing. And the baby. What was he meant to do with the baby now?

"Put him on her belly," Koti said urgently. "Against her skin. To stay warm."

"Uh…" Drew had both hands around the baby, and Koti was the one who gently pulled Hannah's dress further up her body, bared her from the breast down, so Drew could place the tiny body, the baby fully wailing now, wriggling angrily, onto her belly.

Her hands came up instantly to cradle him, and the baby quieted, because somehow, he knew her. He knew she had him, and that he was safe.

"The cord, though," Drew told Koti. Because it was still there. Of course it was still there. It had to come out. Didn't it? How did that happen? "Are we meant to cut it?"

"Leave it," Koti said. "They're coming. They'll deal with it. Leave it. He's fine, and so is she. It's all good."

Drew realized that was a siren in the distance, intruding at the edge of his consciousness. And that a bus had pulled up behind him, blowing its horn.

He didn't even look up. Some of the adrenaline was leaving his body now, and he realized that his hands were covered with blood, and Hannah was bloody too. She was shaking. She was cold, and the baby was cold. They shouldn't be cold.

He pulled his T-shirt off with unsteady hands. "Give me your shirt," he told Koti, who got the message immediately, yanked his own shirt over his head, handed it to him.

People were getting off the bus behind the car, and Koti was turning to them, explaining, talking, forming a screen for the little tableau, but Drew barely noticed. He laid his shirt over his son's little body, saw the tiny pursed mouth nuzzling at Hannah's skin, searching for the comfort of her familiar body, and felt a rush of tenderness so strong, it nearly sent him to his knees.

He murmured something, some nonsense that would embarrass him later to recall, covered her as best he could with Koti's shirt, knowing it would matter to her if she registered that the bus passengers—and the driver now, too—were looking, and for when the ambos came.

He covered her, then laid his hand over her own through the fabric, still warm and damp from his own sweating body, that blanketed their baby.

"It's all good, sweetheart," he told her, the siren closer now, thank God. He heard the tremble in his voice, and didn't care. "They're coming to help you. It's all good."

She opened her eyes and looked into his, and smiled with so much fatigue, and so much sweetness. She *smiled.*

"It was the tunnel," she said, her voice thin, shaky, so tired. "We were in the tunnel. But you got to us. You were there, Drew."

"Yeh," he said, and if there were some tears now, he didn't care about that either. "I was there. I'll always be there. Because the dream was wrong. I'll always be there."

rubbish at speeches

♡

Hannah found, afterwards, that the minutes and hours that followed the birth of her third child were hazy in her memory, the scenes seeming to fade in and out.

The uniformed paramedic, his voice soothing, kind, bent over inside the car, shoving Drew out of the way, and she wanted Drew.

Two of them transferring her, baby and all, from the back seat of the car to the gurney, both her hands clutching the little body for dear life, a paramedic's hand on the other side of hers just in case.

The little semicircle of onlookers she hadn't been aware of until then, some of them with their phones held in the air. Not really interested in her, she dimly knew. Photographing Drew and Koti with their shirts off, and a dramatic moment.

It would be on the news, and it should have bothered her, but she couldn't bring herself to care. Drew would handle it. He could handle the police, too, because a couple of them had materialized from somewhere, were standing in front of the little crowd. She didn't have to worry about that.

The men were lifting her into the ambulance then, Drew beside her again, holding her hand, and the doors were closing, and it was quiet again, and that was better.

She barely noticed when they cut the baby's cord, when they asked her to push, when they delivered the placenta. She only knew that her shaking was slowly subsiding under the blanket, that she had the baby at her breast now, that he was sucking, that he was warming up too, and that he was strong. That he was all right.

The siren sounded, loud and piercing, and she wished it would stop. Then the vehicle turned, slowed, and stopped. The doors were opening again, she and the baby were being passed out the back, and Drew was jumping down with her, walking beside her as she was wheeled into the building, down tiled corridors that could never have been anything but a hospital, and into a room.

The baby was being taken from her by capable hands, starting to cry again, but that was all right too, because he was being looked after, and he was still here, still in the room with her, which meant that they weren't worried, and the relief of it melted the last of her tension away. A woman was doing some stitching down below, a doctor or a midwife, Hannah didn't know. She had torn, but that didn't matter. She barely felt it. She was so tired, though. So tired.

"Drew," she said.

He looked down at her. He still had her hand in his, and she realized for the first time that both their hands were dark red with drying blood.

"What is it, sweetheart?" he asked.

She turned her head so she could see him better. His face, that could look so fierce, so frightening, held only gentleness and concern now. His face made her choke up.

"That was scary," she said. It wasn't nearly enough to say, but she was too tired.

He laughed a little. "Yeh. That was. We had a baby in a car."

"Oh," she realized with distress. "Oh, no. Koti's beautiful car."

"What?" Confusion in the gray eyes now.

"What a...what a mess. It must have been. It must *be.*"

He laughed again. "Sweetheart. He doesn't care."

She closed her eyes and sighed. "Tell him you'll pay to have it cleaned."

"Hannah..."

"Please," she murmured, because she was too tired to talk much more. They had the baby in his little cart now, so she didn't have to worry, because he was all right. A nurse was cleaning her up, wiping away the blood that covered half her body, handing Drew more wipes to clean his hands and her own. But she had to say this first. "Tell him. Promise."

"All right," he said, and shifted around, because they were about to wheel her into her room. "We'll get his car cleaned. I promise."

"And, Drew..."

He sighed. *"And* the cinema. I promise."

She reached for his hand once more, smiled a little, though it was wobbly. "Thanks. But it wasn't that. It was...I love you. And...thank you. For being there. For being...mine."

His face worked for a minute, his eyes shining with unshed tears, and his voice, when the words finally came, was husky. "I...me too. I'm so proud of you. You..." He stopped, got himself together with a visible effort. "You did awesome. And I love you."

He stopped again, then laughed, though it came out a little choked. "I'm rubbish at speeches, eh." He bent down, gave her a soft kiss on the mouth, smoothed her hair back with a gentle hand, and she sighed and closed her eyes again and let them wheel her away.

He didn't have to say it. He didn't have to say anything. She knew.

epilogue

♡

The day when Hugh Latimer married Josie Pae Ata turned out to be just about perfect.

A few white clouds traced wispy patterns in an azure sky, their delicate outlines mirrored in the placid waters of Katikati Harbour below. From where she sat in a wooden pew next to a window of the little white church, Reka had a view over green lawns to the teardrop-shaped harbour, and all the way across it to the Pacific stretching beyond.

So peaceful, and so much like her own wedding day. Another tranquil December afternoon with the cicadas buzzing forth their summer song, in a little church at the edge of a quiet town on the sea. The familiar hymns and prayers of the Church of England, a congregation made up of white and brown faces. And the big men in their black suits, turning up as always to support their teammate on this latest adventure.

The organ was playing, and she was tearing up a bit. She put a hand through Hemi's powerful arm in its sober black sleeve, and he turned to her.

"Look at Hugh," she said quietly. "He's over the moon."

Hemi cast an eye over the tall, broad, bearded figure at the front of the church, standing rock-solid beside the shifting form of his little brother, his eyes steady on the back of the church. Watching for Josie.

"He is," Hemi said. "And he's terrified."

She let out a shocked little puff of laughter, and he smiled, brought his hand up to squeeze hers. "As he should be," he assured her. "He wants to do it right. Wants to be the man she needs. If he weren't terrified, he wouldn't care enough."

"We don't need you to be perfect," she said. "We just need you to be there for us, to hold us and love us, and let us love you."

"Yeh," he said, his smile all for her now. "I know. But he's just learning."

The music swelled, and Hugh's sister was walking towards him, her face intent, and Reka's own heart turned over to see Hugh smile at her, make the effort to encourage her.

"He's a good man," she said under her breath.

A squeeze from Hemi's hand was her reply, and the congregation was standing, because here came Josie.

She choked up a little more, because Hugh's face... he looked like everything he needed in this world was walking towards him. And when Josie reached him, and he lifted her veil over her head and smiled down into her eyes, and she smiled back up at him...it was a very good moment.

The congregation took their seats again, and the service began. Just like Reka and Hemi's own, of course, because every Church of England wedding service *was* exactly the same.

There was a reason you went to weddings, though. All that new young hope, that pledging of faith—it reminded you why you'd done it, and that you'd do it again. If you were one of the lucky ones, and she was. She could feel it in the press of Hemi's arm against her hand, the suspicious sheen in his eye, and was filled with an uprush of gratitude for her good life, and her good man.

There were funny moments, too, which was good, or she'd have spent the entire brief service crying. When the priest asked Hugh the questions, and he answered, "I will," and his voice rang out through the little building like he was on the rugby pitch. More than one person jumped, and a ripple of laughter swept through the congregation. Hugh laughed a little too, Josie smiled back at him, and Reka guessed that that had meant something, and was glad for them that it did.

And when it was time for Hugh to put the ring on Josie's finger, and Charlie was meant to produce it—that was a moment and a half. Hugh turned to his brother with a nod, the boy pulled the band from the breast pocket to which his hand had strayed throughout the ceremony—and dropped it.

It rolled. Of course it rolled. The faint sound echoed through the church, then came to a stop when the ring did. Where, Reka couldn't see.

"Sorry." That was Charlie, his voice anguished. "I'm sorry." He was on his knees, searching frantically.

"No worries," Hugh said. He'd already crouched down beside his brother, was hunting at the edge of the altar, running a big hand along the floorboards.

He pounced, and in the next moment, was standing up, facing the congregation with a white grin splitting his darkly bearded face, holding the circle of gold aloft.

Some clapping and cheering broke out, and Hugh dropped a hand to Charlie's head, tousled his brown hair, and then he was turning back to Josie, taking her left hand in his.

When he spoke, nobody was laughing anymore.

"Josie," he told her, his voice ringing out once more, strong and sure, "I give you this ring as a sign of our marriage. With my body I honor you, all that I am I give to you, and all that I have I share with you."

Reka didn't think there was a dry eye in the house. Not Hemi's, and certainly not hers.

♡

"Great wedding," Kate said a couple hours later, sitting back from the table and taking a final bite of cake. "Too bad Hannah's missing it. She's a sucker for this stuff."

Koti laughed. "And you're not, eh. Too tough. And yet I could swear I saw a tear or two there."

"Could be," she conceded.

"Reka went through an entire pack of tissues," Hemi said with satisfaction.

"And handed you one," she pointed out, which got a laugh from everybody.

"It was beautiful," Kristen said. "They looked so happy."

"They did. And I may have teared up a bit there too," Koti admitted. "After yesterday..." He sighed. "I guess I'm still emotional. I've never played a test match as tough as that in my life, and I never will. And I'm not sure that I haven't changed my mind about getting you pregnant again," he told Kate.

"Too late," she said. "I have a feeling you've done the damage."

He stared at her. "You can't know that yet."

"No?" she said. "You wait and see."

He looked stunned, and everybody else was smiling.

"We won't ask when," Hemi said. "We'll show a bit of delicacy."

"So many weddings," Reka said. "It made me wonder, what happens to the Yaris now? I saw it behind Drew and Hannah's garage the other day," she told Kristen. "A bit small for mum and baby, you reckoned?"

"Yeh," Liam said, his arm as usual around the back of Kristen's chair. "Time to retire it."

"It happens," Reka said. "Though for me, it took three babies." She looked at Hemi. "But I won't hold that against you."

"Whoa, whoa, whoa." Kate was holding up a hand. "The Yaris was *yours?* But I got it from Hannah."

Reka looked at Hemi, and they were both smiling.

"Because we weren't allowed to say," Hemi said. "Drew bought it from me to give Hannah when she moved to En Zed. Didn't want her to know where it came from. Or, more likely, how much it cost him. She tended to get a bit stroppy about her independence in those days, eh."

"Those Yank girls can be like that," Koti said with a grin, which made Kate elbow him in the side.

"Rightly so," she told him. "You'd have run right over me otherwise."

"Never," he pronounced. "Never, ever happen."

"So you had it first, Reka," Kate said. "And then Hannah, and then she loaned it to me, and then I got... done with it."

"And then she loaned it to me," Kristen said.

"And me," Ally piped up from beyond Kristen. "I got a speeding ticket in that car. Probably the only one it's ever seen."

"Yeh," Reka sighed with satisfaction. "That little car seems to be a bit of a charm, doesn't it? Almost hate to see her sell it. It's like...the Sisterhood of the Traveling Toyota. Makes you wonder where it'll turn up next."

"Because surely," Hemi said, "there's another pretty girl out there somewhere holding a boarding pass for New Zealand. And another All Black just waiting to take a fall."

The End

Sign up for my New Release mailing list at
www.rosalindjames.com/mail-list to be
notified of special pricing on new books,
sales, and more.

Turn the page for a Kiwi glossary and a
preview of the next book in the series.

a kiwi glossary

A few notes about Maori pronunciation:
- The accent is normally on the first syllable.
- All vowels are pronounced separately.
- All vowels except u have a short vowel sound.
- "wh" is pronounced "f."
- "ng" is pronounced as in "singer," not as in "anger."

ABs: All Blacks
across the Ditch: in Australia (across the Tasman Sea). Or, if you're in Australia, in New Zealand!
advert: commercial
agro: aggravation
air con: air conditioning
All Blacks: National rugby team. Members are selected for every series from amongst the five NZ Super 15 teams. The All Blacks play similarly selected teams from other nations.
ambo: paramedic
Aotearoa: New Zealand (the other official name, meaning "The Land of the Long White Cloud" in Maori)
arvo, this arvo: afternoon
Aussie, Oz: Australia. (An Australian is also an Aussie. Pronounced "Ozzie.")
bach: holiday home (pronounced like "bachelor")

backs: rugby players who aren't in the scrum and do more running, kicking, and ball-carrying—though all players do all jobs and play both offense and defense. Backs tend to be faster and leaner than forwards.

bangers and mash: sausages and potatoes

barrack for: cheer for

bench: counter (kitchen bench)

berko: berserk

Big Smoke: the big city (usually Auckland)

bikkies: cookies

billy-o, like billy-o: like crazy. "I paddled like billy-o and just barely made it through that rapid."

bin, rubbish bin: trash can

bit of a dag: a comedian, a funny guy

bits and bobs: stuff ("be sure you get all your bits and bobs")

blood bin: players leaving field for injury

Blues: Auckland's Super 15 team

bollocks: rubbish, nonsense

boofhead: fool, jerk

booking: reservation

boots and all: full tilt, no holding back

bot, the bot: flu, a bug

Boxing Day: December 26—a holiday

brekkie: breakfast

brilliant: fantastic

bub: baby, small child

buggered: messed up, exhausted

bull's roar: close. "They never came within a bull's roar of winning."

bunk off: duck out, skip (bunk off school)

bust a gut: do your utmost, make a supreme effort

Cake Tin: Wellington's rugby stadium (not the official name, but it looks exactly like a springform pan)

caravan: travel trailer

cardie: a cardigan sweater

CBD: Central Business District; downtown

chat up: flirt with

chilly bin: ice chest

chips: French fries. (potato chips are "crisps")

chocolate bits: chocolate chips

chocolate fish: pink or white marshmallow coated with milk chocolate, in the shape of a fish. A common treat/reward for kids (and for adults. You often get a chocolate fish on the saucer when you order a mochaccino—a mocha).

choice: fantastic

chokka: full

chooks: chickens

Chrissy: Christmas

chuck out: throw away

chuffed: pleased

collywobbles: nervous tummy, upset stomach

come a greaser: take a bad fall

costume, cossie: swimsuit (female only)

cot: crib (for a baby)

crook: ill

cuddle: hug (give a cuddle)

cuppa: a cup of tea (the universal remedy)

CV: resumé

cyclone: hurricane (Southern Hemisphere)

dairy: corner shop (not just for milk!)

dead: very; e.g., "dead sexy."

dill: fool

do your block: lose your temper

dob in: turn in; report to authorities. Frowned upon.

doco: documentary

doddle: easy. "That'll be a doddle."

dodgy: suspect, low-quality

dogbox: The doghouse—in trouble

dole: unemployment.

dole bludger: somebody who doesn't try to get work and lives off unemployment (which doesn't have a time limit in NZ)

Domain: a good-sized park; often the "official" park of the town.

dressing gown: bathrobe

drongo: fool (Australian, but used sometimes in NZ as well)

drop your gear: take off your clothes

duvet: comforter

earbashing: talking-to, one-sided chat

electric jug: electric teakettle to heat water. Every Kiwi kitchen has one.

En Zed: Pronunciation of NZ. ("Z" is pronounced "Zed.")

ensuite: master bath (a bath in the bedroom).

eye fillet: premium steak (filet mignon)

fair go: a fair chance. Kiwi ideology: everyone deserves a fair go.

fair wound me up: Got me very upset

fantail: small, friendly native bird

farewelled, he'll be farewelled: funeral; he'll have his funeral.

feed, have a feed: meal

first five, first five-eighth: rugby back—does most of the big kicking jobs and is the main director of the backs. Also called the No. 10.

fixtures: playing schedule

fizz, fizzie: soft drink
fizzing: fired up
flaked out: tired
flash: fancy
flat to the boards: at top speed
flat white: most popular NZ coffee. An espresso with milk but no foam.
flattie: roommate
flicks: movies
flying fox: zipline
footpath: sidewalk
footy, football: rugby
forwards: rugby players who make up the scrum and do the most physical battling for position. Tend to be bigger and more heavily muscled than backs.
fossick about: hunt around for something
front up: face the music, show your mettle
garden: yard
get on the piss: get drunk
get stuck in: commit to something
give way: yield
giving him stick, give him some stick about it: teasing, needling
glowworms: larvae of a fly found only in NZ. They shine a light to attract insects. Found in caves or other dark, moist places.
go crook, be crook: go wrong, be ill
go on the turps: get drunk
gobsmacked: astounded
good hiding: beating ("They gave us a good hiding in Dunedin.")
grotty: grungy, badly done up

ground floor: what we call the first floor. The "first floor" is one floor up.

gumboots, gummies: knee-high rubber boots. It rains a lot in New Zealand.

gutted: thoroughly upset

Haast's Eagle: (extinct). Huge native NZ eagle. Ate moa.

haere mai: Maori greeting

haka: ceremonial Maori challenge—done before every All Blacks game

halfback: No. 9 in rugby. With the first-five (No. 10), directs the game. Also feeds the scrum and generally collects the ball from the ball carrier at the breakdown and distributes it.

hang on a tick: wait a minute

hard man: the tough guy, the enforcer

hard yakka: hard work (from Australian)

harden up: toughen up. Standard NZ (male) response to (male) complaints: "Harden the f*** up!"

have a bit on: I have placed a bet on [whatever]. Sports gambling and prostitution are both legal in New Zealand.

have a go: try

Have a nosy for…: look around for

head: principal (headmaster)

head down: or head down, bum up. Put your head down. Work hard.

heaps: lots. "Give it heaps."

hei toki: pendant (Maori)

holiday: vacation

honesty box: a small stand put up just off the road with bags of fruit and vegetables and a cash box. Very common in New Zealand.

hooker: rugby position (forward)

hooning around: driving fast, wannabe tough-guy behavior (typically young men)

hoovering: vacuuming (after the brand of vacuum cleaner)

ice block: popsicle

I'll see you right: I'll help you out

in form: performing well (athletically)

it's not on: It's not all right

iwi: tribe (Maori)

jabs: immunizations, shots

jandals: flip-flops. (This word is only used in New Zealand. Jandals and gumboots are the iconic Kiwi footwear.)

jersey: a rugby shirt, or a pullover sweater

joker: a guy. "A good Kiwi joker": a regular guy; a good guy.

journo: journalist

jumper: a heavy pullover sweater

ka pai: going smoothly (Maori).

kapa haka: school singing group (Maori songs/performances. Any student can join, not just Maori.)

karanga: Maori song of welcome (done by a woman)

keeping his/your head down: working hard

kia ora: welcome (Maori, but used commonly)

kilojoules: like calories—measure of food energy

kindy: kindergarten (this is 3- and 4-year-olds)

kit, get your kit off: clothes, take off your clothes

Kiwi: New Zealander OR the bird. If the person, it's capitalized. Not the fruit.

kiwifruit: the fruit. (Never called simply a "kiwi.")

knackered: exhausted

knockout rounds: playoff rounds (quarterfinals, semifinals, final)

koru: ubiquitous spiral Maori symbol of new beginnings, hope

kumara: Maori sweet potato.

ladder: standings (rugby)

littlies: young kids

lock: rugby position (forward)

lollies: candy

lolly: candy or money

lounge: living room

mad as a meat axe: crazy

maintenance: child support

major: "a major." A big deal, a big event

mana: prestige, earned respect, spiritual power

Maori: native people of NZ—though even they arrived relatively recently from elsewhere in Polynesia

marae: Maori meeting house

Marmite: Savory Kiwi yeast-based spread for toast. An acquired taste. (Kiwis swear it tastes different from Vegemite, the Aussie version.)

mate: friend. And yes, fathers call their sons "mate."

metal road: gravel road

Milo: cocoa substitute; hot drink mix

mind: take care of, babysit

moa: (extinct) Any of several species of huge flightless NZ birds. All eaten by the Maori before Europeans arrived.

moko: Maori tattoo

mokopuna: grandchildren

motorway: freeway

mozzie: mosquito; OR a Maori Australian (Maori + Aussie = Mozzie)

muesli: like granola, but unbaked

munted: broken

naff: stupid, unsuitable. "Did you get any naff Chrissy pressies this year?"

nappy: diaper

narked, narky: annoyed

netball: Down-Under version of basketball for women. Played like basketball, but the hoop is a bit narrower, the players wear skirts, and they don't dribble and can't contact each other. It can look fairly tame to an American eye. There are professional netball teams, and it's televised and taken quite seriously.

new caps: new All Blacks—those named to the side for the first time

New World: One of the two major NZ supermarket chains

nibbles: snacks

nick, in good nick: doing well

niggle, niggly: small injury, ache or soreness

no worries: no problem. The Kiwi mantra.

No. 8: rugby position. A forward

not very flash: not feeling well

Nurofen: brand of ibuprofen

nutted out: worked out

OE: Overseas Experience—young people taking a year or two overseas, before or after University.

offload: pass (rugby)

oldies: older people. (or for the elderly, "wrinklies!")

on the front foot: Having the advantage. Vs. on the back foot—at a disadvantage. From rugby.

Op Shop: charity shop, secondhand shop

out on the razzle: out drinking too much, getting crazy

paddock: field (often used for rugby—"out on the paddock")

Pakeha: European-ancestry people (as opposed to Polynesians)

Panadol: over-the-counter painkiller

partner: romantic partner, married or not

patu: Maori club

paua, paua shell: NZ abalone

pavlova (pav): Classic Kiwi Christmas (summer) dessert. Meringue, fresh fruit (often kiwifruit and strawberries) and whipped cream.

pavement: sidewalk (generally on wider city streets)

pear-shaped, going pear-shaped: messed up, when it all goes to Hell

penny dropped: light dawned (figured it out)

people mover: minivan

perve: stare sexually

phone's engaged: phone's busy

piece of piss: easy

pike out: give up, wimp out

piss awful: very bad

piss up: drinking (noun) a piss-up

pissed: drunk

pissed as a fart: very drunk. And yes, this is an actual expression.

play up: act up

playing out of his skin: playing very well

plunger: French Press coffeemaker

PMT: PMS

pohutukawa: native tree; called the "New Zealand Christmas Tree" for its beautiful red blossoms at Christmastime (high summer)

poi: balls of flax on strings that are swung around the head, often to the accompaniment of singing and/or dancing by women. They make rhythmic patterns in the air, and it's very beautiful.

Pom, Pommie: English person

pop: pop over, pop back, pop into the oven, pop out, pop in

possie: position (rugby)

postie: mail carrier

pot plants: potted plants (not what you thought, huh?)

poumanu: greenstone (jade)

prang: accident (with the car)

pressie: present

puckaroo: broken (from Maori)

pudding: dessert

pull your head in: calm down, quit being rowdy

Pumas: Argentina's national rugby team

pushchair: baby stroller

put your hand up: volunteer

put your head down: work hard

rapt: thrilled

rattle your dags: hurry up. From the sound that dried excrement on a sheep's backside makes, when the sheep is running!

red card: penalty for highly dangerous play. The player is sent off for the rest of the game, and the team plays with 14 men.

rellies: relatives

riding the pine: sitting on the bench (as a substitute in a match)

rimu: a New Zealand tree. The wood used to be used for building and flooring, but like all native NZ trees, it was over-logged. Older houses, though, often have rimu floors, and they're beautiful.

Rippa: junior rugby

root: have sex (you DON'T root for a team!)

ropeable: very angry

ropey: off, damaged ("a bit ropey")

rort: ripoff

rough as guts: uncouth

rubbish bin: garbage can

rugby boots: rugby shoes with spikes (sprigs)

Rugby Championship: Contest played each year in the Southern Hemisphere by the national teams of NZ, Australia, South Africa, and Argentina

Rugby World Cup, RWC: World championship, played every four years amongst the top 20 teams in the world

rugged up: dressed warmly

ruru: native owl

Safa: South Africa. Abbreviation only used in NZ.

sammie: sandwich

scoff, scoffing: eating, like "snarfing"

selectors: team of 3 (the head coach is one) who choose players for the All Blacks squad, for every series

serviette: napkin

shag: have sex with. A little rude, but not too bad.

shattered: exhausted

sheds: locker room (rugby)

she'll be right: See "no worries." Everything will work out. The other Kiwi mantra.

shift house: move (house)

shonky: shady (person). "a bit shonky"

shout, your shout, my shout, shout somebody a coffee: buy a round, treat somebody

sickie, throw a sickie: call in sick

sin bin: players sitting out 10-minute penalty in rugby (or, in the case of a red card, the rest of the game).

sink the boot in: kick you when you're down

skint: broke (poor)

skipper: (team) captain. Also called "the Skip."

slag off: speak disparagingly of; disrespect

smack: spank. Smacking kids is illegal in NZ.

smoko: coffee break

snog: kiss; make out with

sorted: taken care of

spa, spa pool: hot tub

sparrow fart: the crack of dawn

speedo: Not the swimsuit! Speedometer. (the swimsuit is called a budgie smuggler—a budgie is a parakeet, LOL.)

spew: vomit

spit the dummy: have a tantrum. (A dummy is a pacifier)

sportsman: athlete

sporty: liking sports

spot on: absolutely correct. "That's spot on. You're spot on."

Springboks, Boks: South African national rugby team

squiz: look. "I was just having a squiz round." "Giz a squiz": Give me a look at that.

stickybeak: nosy person, busybody

stonkered: drunk—a bit stonkered—or exhausted

stoush: bar fight, fight

straight away: right away

strength of it: the truth, the facts. "What's the strength of that?" = "What's the true story on that?"

stroppy: prickly, taking offense easily

stuffed up: messed up

Super 15: Top rugby competition: five teams each from NZ, Australia, South Africa. The New Zealand Super 15 teams are, from north to south: Blues (Auckland), Chiefs (Waikato/Hamilton), Hurricanes (Wellington), Crusaders (Canterbury/Christchurch), Highlanders (Otago/Dunedin).

supporter: fan (Do NOT say "root for." "To root" is to have (rude) sex!)

suss out: figure out

sweet: dessert

sweet as: great. (also: choice as, angry as, lame as... Meaning "very" whatever. "Mum was angry as that we ate up all the pudding before tea with Nana.")

takahe: ground-dwelling native bird. Like a giant parrot.

takeaway: takeout (food)

tall poppy: arrogant person who puts himself forward or sets himself above others. It is every Kiwi's duty to cut down tall poppies, a job they undertake enthusiastically.

Tangata Whenua: Maori (people of the land)

tapu: sacred (Maori)

Te Papa: the National Museum, in Wellington

tea: dinner (casual meal at home)

tea towel: dishtowel

test match: international rugby match (e.g., an All Blacks game)

throw a wobbly: have a tantrum

tick off: cross off (tick off a list)

ticker: heart. "The boys showed a lot of ticker out there today."

togs: swimsuit (male or female)

torch: flashlight

touch wood: knock on wood (for luck)

track: trail

trainers: athletic shoes

tramping: hiking

transtasman: Australia/New Zealand (the Bledisloe Cup is a transtasman rivalry)

trolley: shopping cart

tucker: food

tui: Native bird

turn to custard: go south, deteriorate

turps, go on the turps: get drunk

Uni: University—or school uniform

up the duff: pregnant. A bit vulgar (like "knocked up")

ute: pickup or SUV

vet: check out

waiata: Maori song

wairua: spirit, soul (Maori). Very important concept.

waka: canoe (Maori)

Wallabies: Australian national rugby team

Warrant of Fitness: certificate of a car's fitness to drive

wedding tackle: the family jewels; a man's genitals

Weet-Bix: ubiquitous breakfast cereal

whaddarya?: I am dubious about your masculinity (meaning "Whaddarya...pussy?")

whakapapa: genealogy (Maori). A critical concept.

whanau: family (Maori). Big whanau: extended family. Small whanau: nuclear family.

wheelie bin: rubbish bin (garbage can) with wheels.

whinge: whine. Contemptuous! Kiwis dislike whingeing. Harden up!

White Ribbon: campaign against domestic violence

wind up: upset (perhaps purposefully). "Their comments were bound to wind him up."

wing: rugby position (back)

Yank: American. Not pejorative.

yellow card: A penalty for dangerous play that sends a player off for 10 minutes to the sin bin. The team plays with 14 men during that time—or even 13, if two are sinbinned.

yonks: ages. "It's been going on for yonks."

Find out what's new at the ROSALIND
JAMES WEBSITE.
http://www.rosalindjames.com/

"Like" my **Facebook** page at facebook.com/
rosalindjamesbooks or follow me on **Twitter**
at twitter.com/RosalindJames5 to learn
about giveaways, events, and more.
Want to tell me what you liked, or what I
got wrong? I'd love to hear! You can email
me at **Rosalind@rosalindjames.com**

by rosalind james

Cover design by Robin Ludwig Design Inc.,
http://www.gobookcoverdesign.com/

Made in the USA
Lexington, KY
13 December 2014